Benjy
the
Football Hero

BENJY THE FOOTBALL HERO

Jean Van Leeuwen

pictures by Gail Owens

DIAL BOOKS FOR YOUNG READERS

NEW YORK

Published by
Dial Books for Young Readers
A Division of E. P. Dutton, Inc.
2 Park Avenue
New York, New York 10016

Published simultaneously in Canada by
Fitzhenry & Whiteside Limited, Toronto
Text copyright © 1985 by Jean Van Leeuwen
Pictures copyright © 1985 by Gail Owens
Printed in the U.S.A.
First edition
COBE
10 9 8 7 6 5 4 3 2 1

Library of Congress Cataloging in Publication Data
Van Leeuwen, Jean. Benjy the football hero.
Summary: Benjy discovers that brains work better than brawn
when it comes to beating the other fourth grade
class's football team.
1. Children's stories, American. [1. Football—Fiction.
2. Schools—Fiction.] I. Owens, Gail, ill. II. Title.
PZ7.V3273Bep 1985   [Fic]   84-21459
ISBN 0-8037-0189-6
ISBN 0-8037-0190-X (lib. bdg.)

For my son David,
who has scored many a stupendous touchdown
in his own front yard

———————————————

J. V. L.

1

"One week from today," said Benjy's mother, "at this exact moment, you will be getting on the school bus."

Benjy looked up at the kitchen clock. 8:25. That was the time, all right. He could see himself slowly climbing the steps of the bus, marching off to his doom. The thought made him want to go back to bed.

"How do you feel about going back to school?" asked his mother, picking up her coffee cup.

"Doomed," said Benjy.

His mother looked startled. "Are things that bad at the Steven J. Mackey Elementary School?" she asked.

"Well," said Benjy, and then he stopped. It was hard to explain.

"Blechhh!" said his little sister, spitting out a mouthful of her sticky gray baby cereal.

That pretty much summed up how Benjy felt about school.

"It's just that summer is so short and school is so long," he said. "And I was just getting used to being on vacation, and now it's over."

"I can understand that," said his mother.

"And I hate setting the alarm clock to get up," Benjy continued. "And I like to stay up and watch baseball games on TV, and now you won't let me anymore."

"You're right," said his mother. "I won't let you anymore."

"And then there's homework," said Benjy. Now that he'd gotten started, he found he had a lot to say. "Fourth grade is the first year we get homework, and probably I won't be able to play after school anymore because all I'll be doing is homework all the time."

"It will take time, there's no doubt about it," said his mother.

"And you learn long division in fourth grade too," said Benjy. "And I think I might already have forgotten multiplication." In his mind he could see pages and pages of math problems, all written in some foreign language. "And then there's Mr. Flannagan."

"What about Mr. Flannagan?"

"He's a mean teacher, that's all. If you do a single thing wrong, he makes you copy pages from the dictionary. And you should see his dictionary. It's this big." Benjy raised his hand over his head. "Danny's brother had Mr. Flannagan and one time he had to copy half a page of the dictionary. Forty-seven words. It took him an hour and a half."

"What did Danny's brother do to deserve such a fate?" asked Benjy's mother.

"Nothing," said Benjy. "He was whispering in line or something."

That was going to be the absolute worst part of fourth grade. Benjy was going to have to sit perfectly still at his desk the entire time so as not to get Dictionary. No talking, no moving—no breathing, practically. It was not possible to sit perfectly still at a desk for six hours a day.

"Well," said his mother, "it sounds rough. But into each life a little rain must fall. Look what's happened to my life."

Benjy looked where his mother was looking. At his sister. While they had been talking, Melissa had turned over her cereal dish and now she was finger painting on the tray of her high chair with the gloppy mess. She had also smeared it in her hair. It looked like Benjy's mother was going to have to give her another bath.

His mother's life was kind of rough, Benjy had to admit. Giving baths to babies, doing baby laundry, cleaning up the kitchen after babies—that was all she seemed to do. A long time ago she used to read books. And play the piano. And teach aerobic dancing. But that was before Melissa came along. Melissa had ruined her life.

"What did you have her for, anyway?" Benjy asked.

His mother laughed. "It's not really that bad," she said. "She has some redeeming qualities. Look at that terrific smile, for example."

His sister was beaming at the revolting mess she had made. It was the sloppiest, drooliest smile Benjy had ever seen. And she only had five teeth too. What was so terrific about that?

"And besides," his mother added, "I know she'll grow up, like you did, and life will get easier again."

Benjy wasn't so sure she was going to grow up. She was certainly taking her time about it. She was almost one and a half and she was still eating like a pig and she still couldn't talk so you could understand her and she still destroyed anything that wasn't bolted down or locked up. He had to barricade his room to protect his things from the mad criminal.

That gave Benjy an idea. Why was Melissa still eating this baby food junk, anyway? They ought to help her grow up by feeding her more grown-up foods.

"Do you mind if I try something?" he asked his mother.

"Be my guest," she said. She poured herself another cup of coffee, probably to brace herself for the big cleanup.

Benjy reached for the cereal box and poured out a few Zingies. Zingies were his favorite cereal. Not only did they help you build a better body, but they tasted great too. Benjy liked them dry or with milk, on ice cream, or even in sandwiches. He bet Melissa would like them too.

He put a few on her tray and the rest in his mouth. "Mmm, good," he said in his most cheerful voice.

Melissa picked up a Zingie and put it in her mouth. She thought it over for a minute. Then she made a terrible face. "Uck!" she said.

Oh, well, everyone didn't like Zingies. Benjy went to the pantry and got down the Raisin Dandies and the Roly-Polies. She was bound to like one of those. She loved raisins.

He poured out a little pile of each on her tray.

Melissa looked them over. It reminded Benjy of a TV commercial. Which one was she going to pick? Maybe they could write to the winning cereal company and they would send out a camera crew to photograph Melissa doing her taste test.

"Tell me, Miss Wilkins," said Benjy, pretending he had a microphone in his hand, "which cereal do *you* like best for starting your day?"

Melissa carefully picked out a raisin from the Raisin Dandies pile and started chewing it. For a couple of minutes her fat cheeks worked hard. Then she took out the wet raisin and handed it to her mother.

Well, those raisins always were kind of hard. And she only had five teeth. Sorry, Raisin Dandies people.

Melissa picked up a Roly-Poly and shoved it in. "Gohssh!" she said and spit it out.

Benjy wasn't sure, but he thought she was trying to say "gross."

Then, with a great wave of her hand, she swept both piles of cereal onto the floor.

So much for the TV commercial, thought Benjy.

His mother looked down at the floor. She didn't yell, like she would have if Benjy had done that. She just looked kind of beaten down. "See what I mean about my life?" she said softly.

Benjy nodded. He went to get the dustpan and

brush. It had been his idea, after all, about that dumb taste test.

By the time he finished sweeping, his mother seemed to have recovered. "I know what we can talk about to cheer us both up," she said, smiling. "Your birthday."

"Good idea," said Benjy.

His birthday was coming up in two weeks, on September 15. In some ways it was a bad time to have a birthday. Everyone was thinking about the start of school, and his birthday got kind of forgotten. Also, he was younger than most of the kids in his class. All through the entire third grade, when everyone else was turning nine, he was only eight. But in another way it was good. His birthday was one nice thing that was happening at the same time all the bad things— school and Mr. Flannagan—were happening.

"What kind of party can I have this year?" he asked.

"What kind of party would you like to have?" asked his mother.

It was hard to decide. There were so many good kinds.

"Well," said Benjy, "there's a bowling party."

"Mmm," said his mother. "You've been to a few of those."

"Or a roller-skating party."

"Ah, yes," said his mother.

"Or a video arcade party."

"What's that?" asked his mother.

"That's where you give each kid about ten dollars and they get to play all the games down at the arcade."

"Terrific," said his mother.

"Oh, and then there's a movie party, like Jason had. We went to see that great racing-car movie."

"Mmm-hmm."

"Or a baseball game party. Remember when Danny's father took us all to the Yankee game and bought us as many hot dogs and sodas as we wanted? And Danny threw up in the car on the way home?"

"I remember your telling me all the gory details," said his mother. "Any other ideas? How about flying you and fifteen of your friends to Disneyland for the day?"

Benjy stared at his mother. Was she serious? Sometimes she liked to pull his leg. "Do you mean it?" he asked hopefully.

His mother looked apologetic. "No, I don't mean it. Sorry, Benjy. I was just wondering what ever happened to the old-fashioned birthday party. You know, the kind that takes place in your own home with balloons and games and a birthday cake?"

"Oh," said Benjy. "They're okay when you're little. I mean, they're great then." He didn't want her to think he didn't appreciate all those birthday cakes she'd baked. "But not when you're nine."

"I see," said his mother. She looked resigned, just like she'd looked when his sister threw all the cereal on the floor. "So what kind do you think you want?"

Benjy ran through them all in his mind again. He was kind of tired of bowling parties. Everyone had been having them lately. And roller skating was not his favorite sport. The last time he went to a roller-skating party he'd been practically run over twice by gigantic teenagers who would wipe out anyone who didn't get out of their way. A video arcade party could be good, though. His friend Jason had won a silver pillow that said "Briar's Scotch Whiskey" on it at an arcade. He didn't think he was in the mood for a movie party. Nothing good was playing. But a baseball party could be terrific. All the hot dogs and sodas you could eat, plus maybe his father would buy Yankee yearbooks with pictures of all the players for everyone.

"I think a baseball party," said Benjy.

"That's what I thought you would choose," said his mother. "There are only a couple of problems. One is who will take you. I'm afraid I'm not up to it after a day with Melissa. You will have to convince your father that he wants to take you to a Yankee game."

Benjy knew what she meant. His father wasn't like Danny's father and most of the other fathers he knew. He didn't play catch with Benjy after work or sit glued to the TV set watching baseball games all weekend. He wasn't really too interested in sports.

"What's the other problem?" asked Benjy.

"The car," said his mother. "The station wagon couldn't be trusted to make such a long trip, so you'd have to go in your father's little car. And that means you could only invite three friends."

It wasn't fair. Danny's father had a van. Danny had invited seven friends.

"Well," said Benjy. "Maybe I'll have a video arcade party."

"I hate to break the news to you," said his mother. "But at ten dollars each you could invite only three friends to that too."

Talking about his birthday wasn't cheering him up that much, Benjy realized. In fact, it was beginning to make him feel worse.

"I have an idea," said his mother suddenly. "You could organize your own baseball game. You could have it in the backyard and we could cook hot dogs on the grill, and you could invite as many friends as you want."

"Hey," said Benjy. "That sounds pretty good." He definitely wanted to invite more people because it was more like a party that way, and besides, it was always nice to get all those presents. "And we could even have a birthday cake for dessert."

"I'd be pleased to make another cake," said his mother, smiling. "When would you like to have the party?"

"How about next Saturday?" said Benjy.

"Right after your first three days of school," agreed his mother. "That might possibly take away some of the pain."

"There are only a couple of problems," Benjy said, thinking it over. "It's almost the end of baseball season. Maybe I should make it a football party."

"Fine," said his mother. "What's the other problem?"

"Her," said Benjy, pointing to his sister. Having demolished everything within reach, she was banging on her tray to announce that she wanted to get down. "Can we put her in a cage during the party?"

"I'll see what I can do," said Benjy's mother.

2

Mr. Flannagan had a tree house in his room. If you finished all your work, you could take a book and climb up and lie on the red-and-yellow-striped cushions and read. That was the good news.

The bad news was that he gave so much work that no one could finish it all. Except Cynthia Babcock. The second day of school she finished twenty multiplication problems while Benjy was still on number six. That was because she was gifted. At least, that's what she told everyone. Benjy hated Cynthia Babcock.

It turned out that he remembered how to do multiplication, after all. Even multiplication with two digits. That was the good news.

The bad news was that next week they were going to start on long division. Mr. Flannagan believed in moving right along. Benjy thought it would have been nicer to ease into division slowly. It was hard enough for his brain to get used to being back in school without rushing into new work.

So far the homework wasn't too bad. Just one sheet of math review or picking proper nouns out of a sentence or something like that. It only took about fifteen minutes, so Benjy could still play after school. That was the good news.

There was no bad news about homework. So far.

Fourth-graders got to play a musical instrument. Mr. Maxworthy, the music teacher, brought all the instruments to class and you could pick one. Benjy picked the trumpet. It was shiny and gold and it sounded great when Mr. Maxworthy played it. Benjy was actually going to be up on stage playing in the band for the Christmas concert. That was the good news.

The bad news was that when he tried to play the trumpet, the only sound that came out sounded like a sick sheep.

In three days he hadn't gotten Dictionary yet. In fact, no one had. Mr. Flannagan didn't seem quite as mean as Benjy had expected. He told jokes and he shook hands with everyone in the class at the end of the day and he even had a bulletin board where he put up a picture of the "Student of the Week." Cynthia Babcock had brought in a whole selection of photographs of herself in different poses because she thought she was going to be up there every week, but Mr. Flannagan said you didn't have to get all 100's to be the "Student of the Week," you just had to do your best work. That was the good news.

The bad news was that the dictionary was there on Mr. Flannagan's desk, all right, and it was *big*. The biggest Benjy had ever seen. *Webster's Unabridged,* Mr. Flannagan called it. Jason said that *unabridged* meant it had all the words in the English language inside of it.

Jason was in Benjy's class again, and Alex Crowley wasn't. Alex, who happened to live on Benjy's block, was the worst kid in the school. That was the good news.

The bad news was that Alex still rode on Benjy's bus. He hadn't moved away or gotten eaten by a bear at sleep-away camp over the summer.

All things considered, there seemed to be a little more good news than bad. And there was Benjy's birthday party coming up on Saturday.

Benjy couldn't wait. Even though his mother

hadn't really let him invite as many friends as he wanted. He had planned on inviting twenty-one kids. Counting himself, that would be twenty-two, so it would be like a real football game, with eleven players on a team. But his mother wouldn't go along with it.

"Do you realize how many hot dogs that would be?" she said. "Sixty-six at the very least, if they all eat like you. And there wouldn't be any lawn left when it was over. Not to mention the noise. We could be asked to leave town. I think a reasonable number would be eight."

"Nine," said Benjy. "Then we can have five on a side."

"Well, okay," said his mother.

It turned out that one kid couldn't come. That made eight, which was nine counting himself, which was an uneven number, but Benjy decided that Matthew could be automatic center, since he wasn't a very good football player. He was too fat to run, and he couldn't pass or catch. He blocked pretty well, though. It was hard to get around anyone that big.

Benjy had the teams all figured out. He would be one captain, since it was his party, and he'd take Jason and Danny and Spencer. Adam, who was really the best player, could be captain of the other team, and he'd have Fernando and Henry and Scott.

They were pretty even teams. It should be a good game. It might even turn out to be better than going to see the Yankees.

The party turned out to be great.

It didn't rain, even though it was supposed to. The weatherman said so, and so did the sky when Benjy got up Saturday morning. It was a dull, gloomy gray. All morning Benjy looked out the window, trying to decide whether the sky was darker or lighter than the last time he'd looked. His mother kept saying if it didn't get better by two o'clock, she would call all the mothers and postpone the party until next Saturday. But at five minutes of two the sun came out and it stayed out for the whole party.

The presents were good. Not great, but good. Benjy got two football shirts with numbers on them, his favorite kind. He put on the yellow-and-blue one from Jason right over his birthday-party shirt. He also got a set of art pencils, a football game, a word game, a weird puzzle that he couldn't figure out, a Frisbee, and a model airplane kit. Last year he'd gotten three model airplane kits. Benjy didn't like building models, so that was an improvement.

The food was terrific. Benjy's father stood next to the grill on the patio with his chef's apron on, cooking up a storm. Everyone had three hot dogs and two sodas except Matthew, who had four hot dogs and three sodas. Benjy guessed his mother had given up on the diet she'd had him on last spring. The birthday cake was Benjy's favorite kind, chocolate with white icing. His mother only made it once a year, because no one but him liked it that much. Everyone at the party liked it fine. The whole cake disappeared in about ten minutes.

Even Melissa didn't cause too much trouble. Benjy's mother tried to keep her inside in her playpen, but she made so much noise that his father said they better let her out before someone called the police. Most of the time she wandered around with a half-eaten hot dog sticking out of her mouth. She took all of the pieces out of the football game and scattered them around the yard and left a print of her fat hand in the cake icing, but that was about it. No major damage.

The best part of the party was the football game. The teams really were even. Jason threw a scoring pass to Spencer, and then Adam threw a scoring pass to Scott. Benjy lateraled to Danny, who went around left end for a touchdown, but then Fernando made a great run up the middle to even up the score.

"It's fourteen all," said Adam. They always counted

the extra points even though they couldn't kick them without goal posts. "Time-out! Soda break!"

"No time-outs," argued Jason. "Our mothers will be coming to pick us up soon. Kick off to us."

"Yeah, kick off," said Benjy and Danny.

"Oh, okay," said Adam.

He got ready to kick off. Benjy lined up next to Jason in the middle of the yard to receive. Then he dropped back a few steps. Adam was a good kicker. One of his kicks had gone practically into Benjy's father's vegetable garden.

Matthew snapped the ball. Adam got off another good one, high and long. It was coming straight to Benjy.

"I got it!" he yelled.

Benjy caught it on his fingertips. He bobbled the ball, almost dropping it. But then he tucked it under his arm, next to his stomach, and started running.

Jason was in front of him, blocking out Scott. Benjy cut across toward the sideline, but Fernando was there. Fernando was a pretty good runner. Benjy faked to the outside, then cut back across the field. Fernando chased him. Benjy ran faster. He loved to run. He could feel the wind on his face as he pulled ahead of Fernando, breaking away into the open.

Then suddenly there was Henry, coming at him

from the other sideline. He made a dive for Benjy's legs, but Benjy dodged. Henry hit the ground. Now there was only Adam between Benjy and the goal line.

Benjy didn't stop. His legs were pumping hard, but he wasn't tired. He felt like he could run forever. He headed for the sideline again. Adam chased him, but Benjy knew he couldn't catch him. He was Tony Trumbull, the best running back in the NFL. Or maybe Billy Joe Crockett. Billy Joe Crockett of the Dallas Cowboys was short, like Benjy, but as speedy and slippery as greased lightning.

Adam tried to tackle him from behind, but Benjy twisted away. He felt fingertips clutching at his shirt, trying desperately to hold on. And then he was in the end zone.

Benjy held up the ball, like Billy Joe Crockett always did on TV, then slammed it down on the ground. Jason came running up and slapped his hands. "All *right!*" he said. Danny slapped him on the back. "Nice run!"

Benjy couldn't believe it. It had been about a ninety-yard runback. At least it would have been if his backyard was a real football field.

"How was that?" he called to his father, who was still standing next to the grill. It looked like he was cleaning it now.

His father waved. "Super!" he called back.

Benjy still couldn't get over it. Usually he didn't do that well in sports. For the first time in his life he felt like all those pro players on TV must feel. It felt terrific. A ninety-yard runback. Even those guys didn't make one like that every day. Finally he was a sports hero.

"Kick off to us! Hurry up!" Scott was calling.

"No! Soda break! I'm thirsty," said Danny.

"No way!" Adam yelled. "We kicked off to you. You have to kick off to us."

"Sorry, guys," said Jason quietly, grinning. "But look who's here."

Adam's mother was just getting out of her car. Danny's father was right behind her. And another car was turning into the driveway.

It looked like the party was over.

"And the final score," announced Jason, doing his sports-announcer imitation, "is twenty-one to fourteen. The Cowboys have trounced the Raiders here today."

"Not the Raiders, the Rams," said Scott.

"Trounced? You call that trounced?" muttered Adam. "Next time we'll bury you guys."

"Cool game," said Jason. "Cool party, Benjy."

Benjy handed out the party bags and watched everyone leave.

"Well," said his mother, when they were all gone. "Are you glad you decided on a football party?"

"It was the coolest party I ever had," said Benjy.

"I'm delighted to hear it," said his mother.

She went inside to clean up. Benjy walked around, picking up soda cans from the patio and the bushes. There was even one on the bird feeder. When he finished, he found his football and wandered back to the backyard.

He thought he'd been standing about even with the pine tree when he caught the ball. He tossed it up and pretended to catch it again. Then he tucked it under his arm and started running.

In his mind Benjy could see Fernando waiting for him.

"But Wilkins fakes him out with a great move to the outside. Perez won't give up. He's chasing Wilkins down the field. But watch this little guy turn on the speed. He leaves Perez in the dust."

Once again Benjy felt that great feeling of running hard and pulling away, out in front, out in the open. The wind was in his hair, his legs were eating up the yards. He was unstoppable.

"Another tackler comes at him, but Wilkins easily eludes him. This guy is amazing. He could go all the way. Now there is only one defender between Wilkins and the goal line. Again Wilkins reverses field. Big Griffin is pursuing him, but it doesn't look like he's going to catch him. Griffin makes a last-minute grab for Wilkins's shirt, but Wilkins is in the end zone standing up. Touchdown!"

Benjy could hear the cheers rocking the stadium. Once more he held the ball up high, then slammed it to the ground. And then he was surrounded by his teammates.

A football hero. That was what he was going to be this fall.

3

"Can we go shopping after school today?" asked Benjy at breakfast on Monday.

"I think my hearing is failing," said his mother. "Would you repeat that, please?"

"I said can we go shopping today? At the shopping center?"

Benjy's mother was looking at him as if he'd just arrived from outer space. "There must be some mistake. You hate shopping, remember? It wastes your time."

"It does," said Benjy. "But this is different. I have my birthday money to spend."

"Ah," said his mother. "The light dawns."

"Well, can we?" asked Benjy.

"I don't know," said his mother. "I have to take Melissa for her checkup at two. And I was going to finish planting those tulip bulbs this afternoon."

"Please, Mom," pleaded Benjy.

"I never thought I'd hear those words about shopping," his mother said, shaking her head. "I'll tell you what. I'll take you to spend your birthday money if at the same time we do some clothes shopping. You need new pants. All your old ones have no knees."

"Well . . ." Benjy hesitated. His mother drove a hard bargain. Shopping for clothes was the worst. "On one condition," he said finally. "No trying on."

"No trying on," agreed his mother. "Only holding up."

"It's a deal," said Benjy.

All day in school Benjy thought about what he was going to buy with his birthday money. He made a list in the margin of the spelling test Mr. Flannagan had just given back:

> football helmet
> shoulder pads
> Cowboys jacket
> Cowboys sweat shirt
> Cowboys belt buckle
> electronic football game
> Billy Joe Crockett poster

During social studies he erased the jacket and the electronic football game. They were bound to be too expensive. He only had $12. He'd gotten $5 from his grandmother in Oregon who had sent him pajamas too; $5 from his Aunt Ruthie; and $2 from his mother's friend who wasn't really his aunt, Aunt Sarah. Maybe he could ask for electronic football for Christmas.

After recess he added "Cowboys wristwatch." Adam had a Steelers one, and he was a great passer. Maybe it was because of his watch.

During math Benjy tried to decide which he wanted most—a new football helmet to replace the one his mother had bought him at a garage sale that was beat up and didn't even have a team insignia on it or a Cowboys sweat shirt or a wristwatch. He couldn't get them all, he knew that. Probably the watch would be too expensive too.

He'd just about decided on the helmet when he noticed that Mr. Flannagan was staring at him with his sharp blue eyes. That was bad. Everyone knew when Mr. Flannagan stared at people he was thinking of giving them Dictionary.

Benjy quickly looked down at his math paper. He was supposed to be doing the ten long division problems on the blackboard. Cynthia Babcock, in front of him, had already finished and was waving her hand in the air to show how gifted she was. Benjy was still on the first problem. He hadn't even been listening too hard when Mr. Flannagan explained how to do it.

Carefully Benjy slipped the spelling test with his list on it inside his notebook. Then he went back to the first math problem. How in the world did you divide 480 by 12?

"Does she have to come too?" Benjy asked.

Melissa was bouncing up and down, smiling like crazy, full of new energy from her nap. Benjy knew what that meant. It meant trouble.

"Of course she has to come too," his mother answered. Of course. She never went anywhere without Melissa these days. That was what was ruining her life.

"Don't worry, Benjy. She'll be in the stroller, and I'm taking plenty of things to keep her busy." His mother had the bag packed that she always took when the baby went anywhere. It had books and toys, little packages of crackers, little boxes of raisins, Melissa's teddy bear, and—the last resort—a bottle of apple juice. Benjy's mother called it her "goodie bag." Benjy thought of it as her defensive weapons.

"Well, we better get going," his mother said.

Benjy helped load Melissa's equipment into the car: her car seat, her stroller, another bag containing diapers and a complete change of clothing in case of emergency, the raggedy blanket that she carried everywhere, and the goodie bag. It looked like they were going on a trip.

"What stores did you want to go to?" Benjy's mother asked on the way to the shopping center.

It was a big mall. There were three whole floors of stores. Benjy didn't even know what they all were. "All of them," he said.

"Well, let's start at Farrell's," said his mother. That was the department store where she always bought his clothes.

"Okay," said Benjy. He might as well get the clothes shopping over with.

He got it over with in about five minutes.

"How about these?" asked his mother, holding a pair of blue corduroy pants up to his legs.

"Fine," said Benjy.

"And some green and brown ones just like them?"

"Okay," said Benjy.

"Are you sure? I know you'll never wear them if you don't like them."

"I'm sure," said Benjy.

That was that. The pants were the same size as his

old ones, he was sorry to see. He'd been hoping he'd grown a little over the summer.

While his mother paid for the pants, Benjy wandered around the boys' department. He thought he remembered seeing baseball sweat shirts there last spring. Maybe they had football ones now.

He walked around a corner and stopped. There was a big circular rack just loaded with NFL team stuff—jackets and bathrobes and running suits and long-sleeve shirts and, way at the end, sweat shirts.

"Oh, boy!" said Benjy. He went right to the sweat shirts.

There were the Giants and the Jets and the Falcons and the Steelers and the Dolphins, all in his size. No Cowboys, though.

"Mom, can you help me look?" he asked. "I want the Cowboys."

His mother came over. "Here you are," she said, pulling one out. But it was a bathrobe. Benjy didn't want a Cowboys bathrobe. You couldn't wear that to school.

"I only want a sweat shirt," he said.

They kept looking. They found a Cowboys jacket, but it was $39.95. And a Cowboys running suit, but it was too small. Finally Benjy's mother asked the salesclerk.

"I'm sure I saw one somewhere," she said, and she went to look on another rack. In a minute she came back, carrying a Cowboys sweat shirt.

"Great!" said Benjy. He put it right on. It felt a little big. He went to look in the mirror. The sweat shirt came down almost to his knees, covering up his shorts. In fact, it looked kind of like a dress.

"It's a size fourteen," said the salesclerk. "I'm afraid it's the last one we have."

"Well," said his mother, "you could grow into it."

That might take several years at the rate he was going.

"Why don't we look in some other stores?" his mother suggested. "We can always come back."

Benjy wasn't sure. It *was* a Cowboys sweat shirt, and maybe he would start growing fast all of a sudden. He hated to lose it. What if someone bought it while he was looking in other stores?

"I'll tell you what I'll do," said the salesclerk, smiling. "I'll put it aside for you until we close at five thirty. If you don't come back for it by then, I'll put it back on the rack."

"Well, okay," said Benjy.

Reluctantly he took off the Cowboys sweat shirt.

"Where to next?" asked his mother.

There was a sports store on the second floor, Benjy

remembered. It was called The Complete Athlete. It was bound to have football stuff. "Upstairs," he said.

A poster caught Benjy's eye on the way to the escalator. It was of three pro football players. "Meet the Jets!" the poster said. "Bad Bosley Hicks, Jack Tilley, and Terry Devine will be here at the fountain in person, Tuesday, September 18, at 7:30 P.M. Come and meet the pros and get their autographs!"

Tuesday, September 18—that was tomorrow night. That would really be something, to meet the pros and get their autographs, even if they were on the Jets instead of the Cowboys. Benjy started to show the poster to his mother, but then he changed his mind. She would never bring him, not at 7:30 P.M., Melissa's bedtime. His father probably would just be getting home from work. But he bet Jason's mom would go. Terry Devine, quarterback of the New York Jets, was Jason's favorite player. Wait till he told him.

"Benjy, can you give me some help?" asked his mother.

"Sure," said Benjy.

It was a job getting the stroller and all of Melissa's equipment onto the escalator, but they did it. Melissa seemed to be having a great time. She had her teddy bear clutched in one arm and her blanket in the other, and she was reading books, telling everyone they passed that this was a "guck" and that was a "gorky."

The Complete Athlete really did have everything. Baseball bats and hockey sticks, ice skates and fishing poles, basketball hoops and bowling balls. And about a hundred kinds of sports shoes. Benjy went right to the football helmets. There was a whole row of them lined up in different colors: blue and white, green and gold, red and black. They looked professional.

They were. They were meant for high school kids or older. They were $24.95.

"Don't you have any other helmets?" Benjy asked the man behind the counter.

"We don't carry toys," he said.

The shoulder pads were the same. Maybe Matthew would be big enough to wear them, being almost as big as a high school kid. But not Benjy. He'd fall over. And they were $17.95.

"Do you have any team sweat shirts?" Benjy asked.

"Only in large sizes," said the man.

"How about football posters?"

The man shook his head. "Try Party Tyme on the third floor."

Benjy could see where The Complete Athlete might be great if you were a grown-up. For a kid, it was incomplete.

One thing they did have, though, was wristbands.

Most of the pros on TV seemed to wear something on their wrists—football, baseball, basketball, and tennis stars. Benjy wasn't sure what they were for, but they looked great. And they were only $1.50. He definitely had to have them.

Benjy picked out a pair of red, white, and blue ones, and paid the man with his two dollars from Aunt Sarah. Slipping them on, he went to show his mother.

"Snazzy," she said. "But what are they for?"

"All the pros have them," said Benjy.

"I've got it!" she said. "They're so your hands won't fall off."

His mother had a weird sense of humor sometimes. He quickly changed the subject. "Let's go to the third floor," he said. "I want to look at football posters."

They got on the up escalator. Benjy couldn't believe Melissa. Now she was happily eating raisins and waving to everyone she saw.

On the way to Party Tyme they passed another children's clothing store. But the only sweat shirts they had were plain gray.

Tony Trumbull was in the window of Party Tyme, racing down the field for a score. It was one of the posters Jason had in his room. If they had Tony Trumbull, they must have Billy Joe Crockett too.

The saleslady didn't know if they did or not.

"You'll have to look in the bin," she told Benjy.

The bin was huge. It had posters of rock stars and movie stars mixed in with the sports stars.

"Let me know when you're ready," his mother said. "I'll be looking at birthday cards."

Benjy found Rocco Corelli, the soccer star, and Molly McGrath, the tennis star, and Marty Fox, his second favorite baseball star. This was terrific. If he could just find Clyde Johnson, his favorite baseball star, and Billy Joe Crockett, he could get two posters. They were only $3.50 each.

He kept looking. There was Legs Brown, the basketball star. And J. J. Fortune. What kind of star was he? He was wearing a helmet, but that looked like a guitar in his hand. He must be a rock star.

"Now, Melissa," he heard his mother saying, a couple of aisles away, "you may look but you mustn't touch."

There was Johnny Hopkins, the Cowboys quarterback. And Tony Trumbull again.

"Melissa, what did I tell you? Come down from there. Oh, no!"

There was a terrible crash, and then a wail like a fire engine's siren.

He should have known it was too good to last. Benjy didn't want to know what kind of trouble his sister had gotten into. He kept going through the posters.

"Benjy!" His mother appeared, looking harried. "Melissa saw a stuffed frog she liked and tried to scale a mountain of birthday cards to get to it. She knocked over a rack of puzzles on the way up. I'm putting everything back now. Can you finish up fast so we can get out of here?"

"Okay," said Benjy. He hurried through the posters. José Lopez, the ace pitcher. Terry Devine. The Vegetables, a rock group who all had green hair. And Billy Joe Crockett!

Now all he had to find was Clyde Johnson.

"Benjy!" His mother appeared again, looking desperate. "She just threw all the Halloween masks on the floor. I've got to get her out of this store."

Benjy could see she was right. His mother had Melissa strapped into the stroller like a tied-up chicken ready for the oven. She wouldn't sit like that for long, Benjy knew. In a minute there would be an explosion heard for miles around.

"I've got to find one more poster," Benjy said. "Can't you wait for me outside?"

"Well," said his mother doubtfully, "I've got one package of crackers left. That should give you about five minutes."

Benjy raced through the rest of the posters. Steve Dickey, the hockey star. Melanie Forrest, a girl whose body seemed to consist only of legs and long blond hair. She looked like she had no clothes on. Benjy didn't know what kind of star she was. José Lopez again.

And that was it. He'd been through the whole bin. There was no Clyde Johnson.

But he did have Billy Joe Crockett. He could get Tony Trumbull too. Or maybe Marty Fox.

He couldn't decide. Did he want the posters, or would he rather have the Cowboys sweat shirt? He couldn't go look in any other stores, since Melissa was about to have a breakdown.

Maybe he should try on the sweat shirt again. See if it was really that big. That was what he'd do.

His mother was surprised that he hadn't bought a poster.

"I decided to try on the sweat shirt again," Benjy said.

He and his mother both looked at Melissa. She was sucking on a cracker and hugging her teddy bear. She seemed pretty calm.

"Okay," said his mother. "But you'll have to be really fast."

They took the escalator back to the first floor.

"Did you decide to take it?" the saleslady at Farrell's asked.

"I want to try it on again," said Benjy.

He studied himself in the mirror. It was a great sweat shirt, except for how long it was. But he wouldn't be wearing it with shorts, so maybe it wouldn't look so long. It would really keep him warm, that was another good thing.

But the sweat shirt was $9.99. If he got it, he couldn't get Billy Joe Crockett. If he had Billy Joe Crockett over his bed, it would inspire him to great things. He still couldn't decide.

"No-no, Melissa."

Uh-oh. His time was running out. Melissa was trying to hand her soggy cracker to another baby. The other baby didn't want it. Now Melissa was smearing it on the other baby's blanket.

"Oh, I'm terribly sorry," Benjy's mother was saying to the other baby's mother. "Let me help you clean that up."

Benjy knew what she was going to say to him. They had to go home right this minute. But he couldn't go home. He had to look at the posters one more time.

"Hey, Mom, I'll be right back. Wait here a second, okay?"

Before she could answer, Benjy raced out of the store. On the up escalator he tried to remember where Party Tyme was. The second floor or the third? He thought it was the third.

Luckily the posters were still where he'd left them. Billy Joe Crockett looked great. Should he get him? Or should he get the sweat shirt?

He could wear the sweat shirt to school. The poster would have to stay home. The sweat shirt would probably help him do well in football at recess. With both the sweat shirt and the wristbands, he would be a star.

"The store is closing," announced someone up front. "Please bring your purchases to the register."

Oh, no. It must be five thirty. The lady at Farrell's wouldn't save the sweat shirt for him anymore. She'd put it back on the rack.

Benjy raced out of the store, dodging people like tacklers on a football field. But at the escalator he had to slow down. Now everyone was going down. It had to be five thirty.

"Pardon me," he said to a lady who was crushed against him. Her perfume was about to make him pass out. "Do you know what time it is?"

"Five twenty-seven," she said.

He squeezed past her, slipped around a stroller,

and jumped off the escalator. Once in a while it was useful to be small.

Farrell's was still open. But the salesclerks were counting up their money and putting things away.

"Is it still here?" Benjy asked breathlessly when he got to the boys' department.

"Sure is," said the salesclerk, smiling at him.

"I'll take it," said Benjy.

He gave her all the rest of his birthday money. Without his even asking, she cut off the tags so he could wear it home.

Benjy put on the Cowboys sweat shirt. It felt great. He looked for his mother to show her. But he didn't see her. Where was she, anyway?

"Oh, no! You wouldn't do that, Melissa."

There was a horrendous crash.

Benjy didn't have the heart to look. He'd find out soon enough.

"Benjy, there you are," said his mother. She looked like a total wreck. "Did you hear that? An entire place setting for six, on the floor. Luckily the salesman and I caught the glassware."

Melissa was lying back in the stroller, drinking her last-resort bottle of apple juice, looking pleased with herself.

"Well, I see you decided," said his mother. She

didn't seem to care very much, Benjy noticed. She only had one thing on her mind. "Can we go home now?"

"Yes," said Benjy. "We can go home now."

4

The minute Benjy put on the Cowboys sweat shirt the next morning, he knew he'd made the right choice. With his jeans the sweat shirt didn't look so big. It still came to his knees and he had to turn up the sleeves a couple of times so his hands would show, but that was okay. Looking in the mirror, he thought he looked kind of like Billy Joe Crockett. Remembering his ninety-yard run, he felt kind of like Billy Joe Crockett. The Cowboys sweat shirt was just what he'd been needing. With it he was going to become a star.

He couldn't wait to play football again.

"Cool sweat shirt," said Jason on the bus. "But aren't you a little hot?"

Benjy had to admit he was. The temperature was

supposed to go to eighty today, the weatherman had said. Jason was wearing shorts and a Yankee T-shirt. But Benjy didn't care. He wasn't going to take off his Cowboys sweat shirt even if the temperature went to a hundred. "Hey, Jason," he said. "Want to play football at recess today?"

"Sure," said Jason. "We can cream Adam again."

It seemed to Benjy that recess would never come. To pass the time he started making out his Christmas list on the back of yesterday's math homework. He'd thought of a few things to add:

> football helmet
> shoulder pads
> Cowboys jacket
> Cowboys running suit
> Cowboys wristwatch
> Cowboys duffel bag
> Cowboys sleeping bag
> Cowboys belt buckle
> electronic football game
> Billy Joe Crockett poster
> Clyde Johnson poster
> official NFL football
> NFL team book
> football cards

"What are the seven continents of the world? Can you tell us, Benjy?"

Benjy looked up, startled. Mr. Flannagan's eyes that saw everything were on him. Had he seen what Benjy was doing? If so, he'd get Dictionary for sure. He'd have to stay in at recess and copy words instead of scoring touchdowns. Benjy covered his Christmas list with his elbow. What was the question? Oh, yes, the continents.

"Uh, North America," began Benjy. "South America. Africa."

That was three. What were the rest? Jennifer next to him, who was smart but didn't have to keep telling everyone about it, was whispering something. But Benjy couldn't hear her. Other hands were popping up all over the room. Benjy had to finish. Otherwise Mr. Flannagan would think he didn't listen in class.

"Europe. Asia. Ummm, Antarctica."

There was one more. But what was it? Cynthia Babcock was practically falling out of her chair in front of him, waving both hands in the air.

Mr. Flannagan was doing something strange. He was jumping up and down next to his desk, kind of like a kangaroo.

"Australia!" said Benjy.

"Hooray," whispered Jennifer.

"Thank you, Benjy," said Mr. Flannagan, smiling. "Now, who can name the five oceans of the world?"

Whew! He'd made it. Just barely. But if he was going to make it out to recess, he'd better start paying attention to social studies.

Recess finally came.

"Hey, Adam!" yelled Jason across the playground. "Ready to get really trounced? We challenge you to another game, same teams as Benjy's party."

"Okay," said Adam. "If you're ready to get wiped out."

But they couldn't have the same teams because Fernando was absent.

"See who else you can get from your class," said Jason. "I'll see who I can get from ours. Benjy, you get the ball. We'll meet you on the lower field."

Benjy went to the gym to find a ball. When he got down to the lower field, Adam and Jason were standing in a circle of kids, arguing.

"The teams aren't fair," Jason was protesting. "Look who you've got."

Benjy looked. Besides Scott and Henry and Adam from Mrs. Rinaldi's class, there was Eddie Spaghetti. That wasn't his real name. Jason called him that because he was a big eater, like Matthew. But on Eddie all that food turned to muscle, not fat. He was good in just about every sport. And Mark Moskowitz. He was good too. He always scored the most goals in soccer. And Alex Crowley.

Oh, no. Why did Adam have to get him? Alex Crowley was always trying to wreck Benjy's life. If Benjy did something good, Alex said it stunk. If Benjy did something bad, Alex laughed. He was also huge. That was because he'd repeated first grade. He was going to be ten in November.

"And look who we've got," said Jason.

Jason sure hadn't done too well finding people. The only ones he'd been able to get besides Danny and Spencer and Benjy and himself were Matthew and Kelly Kramer. Matthew couldn't do anything, and Kelly Kramer was a girl.

"No girls allowed in this game," said Spencer.

"Who says?" Kelly had her hands on her hips and there were dots of bright pink on her freckly cheeks. She was tough. Benjy wouldn't want to mess with her. It was an actual fact that she'd beaten up a fifth-grade boy.

"We better let her play," said Henry. She'd pushed him into the sandbox once in first grade, Benjy remembered.

"You can have her, then," Jason said. "We'll trade you Kramer for Spaghetti."

"No way," said Scott. "It's class teams, remember? She's in your class, you've got to keep her."

"Look, it's six against six," said Adam. "That's fair. Are we going to waste the whole recess arguing or are we going to play?"

"Play," said Danny.

"Play," said Benjy. He couldn't wait any longer to try out his Cowboys sweat shirt.

"All right," said Jason. "But I'm playing under protest."

Jason was right. The teams weren't fair. The Rinaldi team had all the big guys except for Matthew, and he didn't count because he couldn't move. You could run right around him. They had the best passer. Adam could really throw the long bomb. And they had Mark Moskowitz, who could do everything.

Every time they got the ball they scored. In the first five minutes they had two touchdowns.

The Flannagan team, on the other hand, was stopped cold. When Jason tried to pass to Spencer, the ball was knocked down by Alex. When Danny tried to go up the middle, he was smothered at the line of scrimmage by Eddie Spaghetti. And Benjy's ninety-yard runs were going nowhere. When he went around left end, he was stopped by Mark. And when he faked to the left and swept wide to the right, he was stopped by Mark. That kid was quick. No matter where Benjy went, he was there.

Benjy couldn't believe it. What was going wrong? Why couldn't he break free for the big run like he had at his party? His Cowboys sweat shirt, which was supposed to make him a star, didn't seem to be working.

"That Moskowitz is like an insect. You can't get rid of him," Benjy complained in the huddle.

"Yeah, a mosquito. Mark Mosquito—that's his name!" Jason loved to give people names. "Hey, Mosquito," he yelled to Mark, who was down on one knee at the line of scrimmage, getting ready to nail Benjy again. "Bug off!"

"How about giving it to me this time?" Matthew asked hopefully.

Jason didn't answer.

"Give it to me," Kelly said. "Fake to Benjy and give it to me."

"Yeah, maybe," said Jason.

But he faked to Benjy and threw long to Danny instead. The ball was over Danny's head. Alex intercepted it and ran it in for a touchdown.

Now the score was 21–0. There was no doubt about

it, the Flannagan team was getting trounced. And recess was almost over too. There wasn't even time to catch up.

But there was time to score a touchdown. At least they could get on the scoreboard.

"Give it to me," said Kelly again in the huddle. "They'll never expect it."

"Or me," said Matthew.

"I have an idea," said Benjy. "We put two guys on Mark to block him out of the play, and I go around left end. He can't get away from two guys."

"Good play," said Jason. "Matt, after you snap the ball, just kind of fall on the Mosquito. If that doesn't work, Danny, you block him."

Jason clapped his hands, like the quarterbacks did on TV, and the Flannagan team came out of the huddle.

"Ninety-five, forty-three, twenty-two—hike!" he barked.

Matthew snapped the ball, and then fell over. Mark Mosquito disappeared from sight. Jason faked a pass to Spencer, then jammed the ball into Benjy's stomach.

Benjy took off. He sidestepped Eddie Spaghetti, shook off Henry, then turned on the speed. Out of the corner of his eye he saw Scott and cut toward the sideline.

Now there was daylight ahead of him. Benjy started feeling that excitement again, that sureness that he was going all the way. His legs were flying over the grass, leaving everyone behind. No one could stop him now. The Cowboys sweat shirt was bringing him luck after all. He knew it would.

"Oof!" Something like a freight train hit him from behind. His legs shot out from under him, and Benjy went down, his nose in the dirt, the football trapped under him, digging into his ribs.

For a minute he just lay there, catching his breath, breathing dirt. Mark Mosquito had done it again. He must have wiggled out from under Matthew somehow.

But when he finally opened his eyes, it wasn't Mark Mosquito who was sitting on him. It was Alex Crowley.

"Did you think you were going somewhere, squirt?" he said softly with his mean grin.

Benjy closed his eyes again. In the distance he could hear the recess bell ringing. For once he was glad.

5

"I can't stand it," said Benjy to Jason on the way home on the bus. "Sat on by Alex Crowley. That was the worst."

"Yeah," said Jason. "Old Creepy Crowley."

That was the best name Jason had ever come up with, no doubt about it.

"What did he have to play for, anyway?" Benjy went on. "It would have been a good game without him."

"Well," said Jason. "Not that good. We still would have lost."

"That's because of who you got for our team," said Benjy. "Matthew and a girl. You couldn't do better than that? Where was Brian? What about Todd and Jeff?"

"Todd and Jeff are both terrible at football, you know that. And Brian wanted to play soccer. That's all he ever wants to do this year. And that's all the boys in our class. Except for that new kid."

"Oh, yeah," said Benjy. "Him." The new kid was weird. He came from some place in the South, and he talked funny. He looked funny too. He was very tall—taller than anyone in the class except Cynthia Babcock—and he had big ears and feet. Probably he'd trip over them if he tried to run. And he had a funny name. Clayton Case the Third. "You mean Case from Outer Space," said Benjy.

"Hey, that's not bad," said Jason, grinning. "Not bad at all. Well, we could let him play tomorrow. Give him a try. We could use something against those guys."

"That's for sure," agreed Benjy. "How about coming over to my house and practicing a few plays?"

"Can't," said Jason. "My mom said I have to get my homework done right away if I want to go to the mall tonight to see the Jets. We'll pick you up at around seven, okay? Oh, boy, is this going to be cool. We are going to get the autograph of Terry Devine."

Benjy didn't care so much about Terry Devine. He

wasn't nearly as good as the Cowboys quarterback, Johnny Hopkins. But seeing real live pro players up close, in person—that was exciting. "See you at seven," he said.

"Hey, Clyde, how's the boy?" said Benjy.

Clyde was his goldfish, named for Clyde Johnson. Benjy always liked to talk to him when he got home from school. He figured it must be kind of a lonely life, being all by yourself in a bowl all day.

Clyde came over to the side of the bowl and twitched his mouth at him. Benjy could never figure out if he was trying to say something or just practicing his chewing. He hated to admit it, but sometimes Benjy thought that fish food was the biggest thing in Clyde's life.

"Yeah, well, my day wasn't so hot either."

That was putting it mildly. To start out planning to be a football star and end up with Alex Crowley sitting on top of him, whispering mean things in his ear and rubbing his nose in the dirt. Well, Benjy was going to show him. Next time he'd dance right out of Alex's tackle, leaving him sniffing the dirt. And after he'd scored a touchdown, he'd casually flip Alex the ball and say, "What's the matter, Crowley? Got lead in your shoes?"

He was going to be a star, like Billy Joe Crockett.

Benjy did his homework fast. Then he sat and studied the picture of Billy Joe Crockett that he'd cut from a sports magazine and pinned up on his bulletin board. What was his secret? What made him such a great runner, anyway? He wasn't huge and powerful like Tony Trumbull. He didn't run over guys. He just ran around them and between them and sometimes, it seemed, even under them. He had a way of escaping from tackles. Just when you thought he was down, he'd miraculously slip away for another ten yards.

It had something to do with his legs, Benjy thought. He studied them carefully. They were quick and had good balance. And they had all these terrific moves. That was what made Billy Joe Crockett so great. He could stop short suddenly. He could twist away from a tackler. He could turn on the speed and shoot through a hole that was hardly there. And then he could change direction so quickly that the tacklers were all running the wrong way. He was amazing at faking out tacklers.

That was what Benjy needed to be a star—some Billy Joe Crockett moves.

Benjy got his old football helmet from the closet and put it on. He looked in the mirror. The white part wasn't so white anymore. It had dirt and grass stains and purple and green zigzags from the time Melissa escaped from her playpen and discovered his crayons. And the blue stars he'd painted on the sides last year looked a little lopsided. Still, if he squinted his eyes, he thought he looked a lot like Billy Joe Crockett. Especially with his Cowboys sweat shirt and his wristbands. He took his football and went out to the backyard to practice.

He practiced stopping short. He practiced twisting away. He practiced turning on the speed. He practiced changing directions. He practiced faking out tacklers. It was kind of hard faking out tacklers who weren't there, but he pretended. Pretending Alex Crowley was about to tackle him made Benjy twist and shift and change direction very fast.

He practiced short runs up the middle, slipping through tiny holes in the line. He practiced long runs around right end and ninety-yard runs across the whole backyard. He scored seven touchdowns altogether, and he practiced throwing down the ball afterward until he could do it exactly the way he'd seen Billy Joe Crockett do it on TV.

He was just practicing a kind of slithering move across the ground that might get him an extra yard or two after the tackle when his mother rang the bell for dinner.

Benjy stood up. He was a little tired, he noticed. But all in all he felt good. Alex Crowley had better watch out tomorrow. Billy Joe Crockett was going to be playing for the Flannagan team.

"How come you brought Deadly?" Benjy asked Jason as they drove to the shopping mall. Deadly was Jason's pet garter snake. He was carrying him in a canning jar that used to say "Pickles" and now said "Beware of the Poisonous Reptile."

"Ssssh," whispered Jason, gesturing at his mother in the front seat. In a louder voice he asked, "Got your paper for the famous autographs?"

Benjy guessed he didn't want his mother to know about Deadly. "Right here," he said, patting his jeans pocket.

Jason's mother dropped them off at the main entrance to the mall. "I'll pick you up right here as soon as I finish my shopping," she said. "Let's make it at eight o'clock. Have fun."

Benjy and Jason walked toward the fountain in the middle of the mall. It seemed pretty crowded.

"So how come you brought Deadly?" Benjy asked again.

"Oh, you know, he likes to get out and see things once in a while," said Jason. "Meet the pros, get some fresh air."

Deadly wasn't getting much fresh air in the canning jar. Somehow that didn't sound like the real reason to Benjy.

"Come on, Jason," he said.

"You'll see, Benjy," said Jason, smiling mysteriously. "You'll see."

Benjy hated it when people smiled mysteriously.

The farther they walked, the more crowded it was getting. Everyone seemed to be heading for the fountain too. Benjy saw a few kids he knew from school. There were fathers with little kids perched on their shoulders. There was a whole high school football team in uniform, wearing snarling bears on their red-and-white shirts. There were families eating picnics on benches. They looked like they'd been there all day.

"Uh-oh," said Benjy. "Maybe we should have come a little earlier."

"I was afraid of this," said Jason.

They couldn't get any closer. They were up against a wall of people. By craning his neck Benjy could make out a platform off in the distance, near the fountain. On it stood about six guys. None of them was wearing a football uniform, but he could tell right away which ones were the Jets. They were the huge ones in green blazers. The guy in the middle must be

Bad Bosley Hicks, the Jets linebacker. He'd had the most quarterback sacks in the NFL last season. Benjy could see why. He had to be the biggest person he'd ever seen in his whole life. Bad Bosley was scowling, just like on TV. He looked like he ate little kids for breakfast to get in the mood for a game. Next to him was a tall blond guy who was probably Jack Tilley, the Jets tight end. Or could that be Terry Devine, and the one with red hair who was almost normal size was Jack Tilley?

A skinny bald man stepped up to the microphone. He was definitely not a Jet. "Good evening and welcome, all you sports fans," he said in a jolly voice. "I'm delighted to see so many of you here tonight. And do we have a treat in store for you! As manager of the Walnut Creek Mall, it is my great pleasure to introduce to you three men whom you see every weekend on your TV screens. But tonight you're going to have the opportunity to meet them in person."

Benjy kind of wished he was seeing them on his TV screen. At least then they'd show a close-up and he'd know which one was Tilley and which was Devine. They'd have their names on their uniforms.

"And now, the man you'd hate to see coming at you on a Sunday afternoon if you were a quarterback in the NFL—Bad Bosley Hicks!"

Benjy struggled to get a look at him around a man in a Jets jacket with a Jets cap on his head.

Bad Bosley stepped up to the microphone and smiled. That sure was different from on TV. The audience broke into applause. Then he spoke in a voice so soft it was hard to believe it could come from such an enormous person. He talked about how great it was to play for such a great team and how he intended to give a lot of trouble to the quarterbacks in the league this season. And that was all he had to say, he said, because his motto was "Speak softly and carry a big stick."

Everyone started clapping and cheering. In front of Benjy and Jason a little boy bounced up and down on his father's shoulders, waving a Jets pennant. Benjy wished suddenly that he were younger, so someone could hold him on his shoulders.

Jack Tilley talked next. He was the blond one. And then Terry Devine. The boy with the Jets pennant got bored and turned around and waved it in Jason's eyes. "Hey, cut that out," Jason protested. "This is the guy I came to see." The man with the Jets jacket and cap offered him a boost up, but after a minute he had to put him down. "Either you're too old for this," he said, "or I am."

Terry Devine said a few things about how terrific

the Jets team was this year and how he hoped to be seeing everyone again in January—in the Super Bowl. Then it was over. "The players will be happy to sign autographs for about fifteen minutes," announced the bald man over all the cheers. "Then they have to catch a plane. Thank you for coming."

Immediately everyone started pushing toward the platform. Benjy and Jason stayed behind the man with the Jets jacket and cap. He was a pretty good blocker. Maybe he had once been a football player himself. But then they were stopped. There must be about five hundred people between them and the Jets players. Those guys would never be able to sign so many autographs in fifteen minutes. Some other people had decided the same thing. They were looking at their watches and moving toward the exit doors. "We'll be here all night," Benjy heard one man say to his wife. "Only they won't." "But I want a autograph," whined the kid he was dragging away.

Benjy looked at Jason. "What do you think?" he said.

"I think," said Jason, "that I'm getting Terry Devine's autograph."

He had that look on his face that said he would never give up. Slowly he unscrewed the lid of Deadly's canning jar.

"What are you doing?" Benjy couldn't imagine what Jason had up his sleeve this time.

"Watch this," said Jason, grinning. "Just stay close behind me and have your autograph paper ready."

Jason took Deadly out of the jar and put him into his jacket pocket. Carefully he buttoned the pocket so he couldn't get out. Then he said in a loud voice, "He's gone! My snake, Deadly, has escaped! Did you see which way he went? I've got to capture him before it's too late."

Several people turned around and stared at Jason.

Jason tapped the shoulder of the man carrying the little kid with the Jets pennant. They both turned around. "Excuse me," he said, holding up the empty canning jar. "It's my snake, Deadly. He escaped! I think he went this way."

Jason bent over and peered past the man's legs.

Both the man and the little kid looked startled. The man stepped aside.

Jason tapped the woman in front of him. As soon as she heard the words "Deadly" and "snake," she moved out of the way, looking around warily.

A murmur seemed to spread through the crowd. People started looking down at the floor instead of up at the Jets stars. A few more moved toward the exits. "This is the last straw," Benjy heard one woman say to her friend. "Mildred, let's go home."

Now a path opened in front of Jason. "I'm sorry," he kept saying as he worked his way closer to the platform. "It's my snake, Deadly. I think he went this way. Have you seen him?"

Benjy followed right behind, clutching his autograph paper in his hand and mumbling "I'm sorry, excuse me" every couple of minutes.

Suddenly Benjy saw, straight ahead of them, a man in a blue uniform. He was big, not like Bad Bosley Hicks was big, but big enough. It was one of the mall's security guards. And from his frowning face Benjy knew just what he was about to say: "What's going on here?"

"Jason!" he said, pulling on Jason's sleeve.

But Jason had already seen him. "Oops!" he said, pointing. "There goes my snake!" And he went down on his hands and knees, pretending to grab for Deadly.

Benjy dove down for cover too into a tangle of moving legs, shopping bags, baby carriages, picnic baskets, and umbrellas. He tried to follow Jason, but he couldn't see anything. A kid stuck a wad of used bubblegum in his hair. Then he was blocked by a pair of football cleats. It must be one of the snarling bears team. Reversing direction, he just missed being knocked unconscious by a lady's purse.

He crawled along the floor, hoping he was going in

the right direction, mumbling "I'm sorry, excuse me." Finally he spotted open space ahead of him. He had to stand up before he got wiped out by a snarling bear or an old lady.

"Hey, Benjy!"

There was Jason, sitting on the edge of the fountain, calmly holding his canning jar. And back in the jar was Deadly.

"I found him," he said. "Isn't that great?"

Benjy looked around. The security guard was nowhere to be seen. And the crowd seemed to have calmed down. No one was even looking at them.

"Great," said Benjy.

"Ready to get some autographs?" asked Jason. Bad Bosley Hicks was standing just a few feet away.

Benjy had lost his autograph paper somewhere in his trip across the floor, so he asked Bad Bosley and Jack Tilley and Terry Devine if they'd sign his sweat shirt instead. They looked at him kind of funny when they saw it was a Cowboys sweat shirt and Terry Devine said maybe it was illegal, but they did it. Benjy figured this ought to make his sweat shirt luckier than ever.

Jason got Terry Devine's autograph and told him he was a quarterback too, and Terry Devine wished him luck and shook his hand.

Jason held out his right hand as if it were no longer part of his body and gazed at it in awe. "I'm never going to wash that hand again," he sighed.

His mother would see about that, Benjy thought.

Then Jason asked Bad Bosley Hicks if he would sign his autograph on Deadly's canning jar label.

"You sure it's safe?" Bad Bosley asked. He was reading the part of the label that said "Poisonous Reptile."

"It's just a garter snake," said Jason.

"Well, okay," said Bad Bosley. "Hey, this is a first for me. An autograph for a snake."

"Take my word for it, Deadly deserves it," said Jason. He looked over at Benjy and grinned. "Right, Benjy?"

"Right," said Benjy.

6

After meeting the pros, Benjy didn't think the Flannagan team looked like much the next day at recess.

Danny and Spencer seemed so shrimpy. No muscles at all on their skinny toothpick bodies. Matthew looked like a lump of something. Didn't he realize that just being big wasn't enough? You had to be able to move your body. Bad Bosley Hicks could sure show him a few things. Probably he'd knocked over jungle gyms and chewed up swings when he was Matt's age. Then there was Kelly Kramer. The pros would never be desperate enough to have a girl on their team. And Case from Outer Space. The Jets coach would die laughing if he walked out on the field. He reminded Benjy of some sort of weird space bird, with his flapping ears and feet. He'd never be able to get off the ground.

But Case from Outer Space turned out to be a surprise. He didn't trip over his own feet when he ran. And he was so tall that he could bat down some of Adam's long bombs. And best of all, he could catch passes. Jason threw a little wild sometimes, but Case from Outer Space just jumped in the air and reached out his long arms and snagged the football.

He scored two touchdowns at first recess.

"Hey," said Jason. "Where did you learn to catch like that?"

Case from Outer Space grinned. "Georgia," he said.

"Cool," said Jason. "I know what we're going to call you! Case the Ace."

And there was someone else on the Flannagan team who wasn't bad either. Kelly Kramer. After she had asked Jason about a hundred times in the huddle to give her the ball, her cheeks getting pinker and pinker, finally he did. No one on the Rinaldi team expected it, and she cruised down the sidelines for about a twenty-yard gain. Benjy figured it was just a fluke. But when Jason gave her the ball again, she ploughed through the middle for fifteen more.

Kelly wasn't particularly fast, and she didn't have

any tricky moves. She was just tough. When she had the ball, her chin jutted out and her eyebrows came down in a ferocious Bad Bosley scowl and her eyes flashed like fire. Just looking at her was enough to make tacklers get out of her way. Jason started calling her "Killer Kelly."

The one player on the Flannagan team who wasn't doing so well was Benjy. Even with his Cowboys sweat shirt autographed by the pros, even with his new Billy Joe Crockett moves, he kept getting stopped at the line of scrimmage. Or worse, thrown for a loss. It wasn't Mark Mosquito this time, since he was playing soccer. It was Alex Crowley.

Alex Crowley had decided to be Benjy's shadow. Wherever Benjy went, Alex was right there, copying his moves. If Benjy twisted and shifted, Alex twisted and shifted. If Benjy changed direction suddenly, Alex changed direction suddenly. If Benjy stopped short, Alex stopped short. And then he tackled Benjy and sat on him.

When other guys tackled, they just grabbed you around the legs and hung on till you went down. Not Alex Crowley. He liked to jump on your back and crush you to the ground, making sure your face got scrunched hard into the dirt. And he didn't get up for a long time. He always had something to say too. Like: "Hey, peewee, who do you think you are, Tony

Trumbull?" Or: "You'd better go play with the kindergarten kids, Benjy-baby. This league's too tough
for you."

With each tackle Benjy got madder and madder.
More than anything else, he wanted the Flannagan
team to beat the Rinaldi team today.

But it didn't work out that way. With the score
tied, 14–14, and only seconds left till the end of recess, Jason tried a long pass to Case the Ace in the end
zone. Unfortunately the Rinaldi team was ready for
the play. They had Scott and Adam and Alex all
covering Case the Ace. Eight hands went up for the
ball. And the ones that came down with it belonged
to Alex Crowley.

Benjy kicked the dirt with his sneakers all the way
back in from recess. He kicked his chair as he sat
down at his desk.

"Hey, Benjy, it's time for band," said Jennifer.
"Remember?"

Benjy got up again and got his trumpet and his
lunch bag from his locker. They went to lunch right
after band. Walking down the hall with Danny, he
kicked at the cracks in the floor.

"Tough game," said Danny. "But at least we tied
them. Next time we'll win. That kid Case is going
to help our team."

"It would help our team more if Alex Crowley fell in a hole," muttered Benjy.

"Hey, did you see *Revenge of Dracula* last night on TV?" Danny asked, his face brightening.

Benjy shook his head. He didn't like scary movies. They always gave him bad dreams. He kicked at the bottom of his trumpet case, pretending it was the bottom of Alex Crowley.

"Oh, wow, you should have seen the blood dripping from this lady's white dress. And then there was the part where her little dog digs up a bone in the garden. Only it's a *human* bone." Danny laughed.

Once Danny got started on horror movies, there was no stopping him. The whole time they were setting up their music stands and taking out their trumpets, he was telling Benjy about all the movies he'd seen last summer. "There was *Sweet Sister Jennifer*," he recalled happily. "This girl is so quiet and everything that she never has a date, but then all of a sudden she starts paying back all the boys who didn't ask her to the senior prom. One gets set on fire and another one drives his car into a lake and this one kid just dissolves. That was the wickedest. One minute he's standing in the chemistry lab and the next minute all you see is a puddle on the floor."

That would be a good possibility for Alex Crowley,

Benjy thought. Dissolve him into a puddle. The idea cheered him up a little.

Mr. Maxworthy tapped on his music stand with a pencil. "All right, boys and girls, let's see if we can make a little music this morning. May I hear some warm-up scales?"

Benjy and Danny blew a few notes. So did everyone else. It sounded pretty awful. Mr. Maxworthy thought they were going to be able to play three pieces for the Christmas concert in December. Benjy kind of doubted it himself.

Danny leaned over toward him. *"The Revolt of the Guinea Pigs* was really cool," he said. "See, all these guinea pigs are being used for scientific experiments, but something goes wrong and they get an overdose of chemicals. And they start growing bigger and bigger. Pretty soon they are breaking out of their cages. And they bite people, and the people turn into giant guinea pigs. There's this one scene where a woman scientist is feeding some baby guinea pigs and she doesn't know about this, see, because she's in a lab on an island where there is no radio or TV, and she gets bitten on the hand. You see this tiny little bite on her hand and then you see her hand actually grow hair and claws. And then the camera moves up to her face and she has whiskers and this pointy little nose."

Cynthia Babcock tapped Danny on the shoulder. She sat behind them and played the baritone horn very loud. And perfectly, of course. "You're supposed to be warming up," she said in her know-it-all way.

Benjy imagined how Cynthia Babcock would look with whiskers and a pointy little nose.

"All right!" shouted Mr. Maxworthy. "That's enough!" He looked like he'd like to put his hands over his ears. "Now, get out your music for 'The Tenderfoot March.' Let's play just the first four measures."

"The Tenderfoot March" didn't sound like a march at all. It sounded like morning in a barnyard, with squeaks, squawks, and bellows. Mr. Maxworthy brought his hands down.

"No, no! You're not playing together. Let me hear just the woodwinds. Clarinets, flutes, and oboes."

While the clarinets, flutes, and oboes squeaked more or less together, Danny described his favorite movie of the summer, *Invaders from a Far-off Planet*. "This is probably the second grossest, most disgusting movie ever made," he said with a grin. "Some creatures from outer space land here, see, and they're trying to take over the earth, but they're in disguise so they look like everyone else. Only in the end, after they've taken over the police and the army and they're about to attack the White House, they start taking off their disguises. You see them rip open their skin and under it is this weird purple crocodile skin. And this one guy pops out his eyeball, and it rolls across the floor. That was the sickest thing I ever saw. I almost threw up."

Cynthia Babcock tapped Danny again. "Will you be quiet?" she said. "I'm trying to study my musical score."

Benjy was beginning to have a good time. "What's the first grossest, most disgusting movie ever made?" he asked Danny.

"The Green Slime," said Danny. "Haven't you ever seen it? It's been on TV tons of times. Of course, they took out most of the best parts. The green slime is this algae that grows on ponds, but then gradually it spreads so it covers everything—trees and roads and houses. And then it gets inside the houses and gets on people, and nothing can stop it. Not armies or bombs or anything."

"Does anything ever stop it?" Benjy asked. It was an interesting idea. He pictured slime growing over his trumpet and his music stand. He pictured it oozing down the hall. And grabbing Alex Crowley.

"Yeah, some fish eat it," said Danny. "But then they start growing bigger and bigger. . . ."

It couldn't have been the green slime, but all of a

sudden Benjy felt hungry. It had to be almost lunch-time. He looked over at Mr. Maxworthy. He was working with the percussion section now, trying to convince Josh, a big sixth-grader, that a bass drum could be played quietly. No one would notice if Benjy snuck a little bite of his lunch.

Benjy felt around in his bag until he found his sandwich. The smell told him it was peanut butter and jelly, his favorite. That was a relief. Sometimes his mother gave him something else for a change, like egg salad with bean sprouts. Her kind of change he could do without.

"So this one policeman says to the other one, 'Giant ants? You've got to be kidding.' And then he turns around and you see these enormous antennae in the rearview mirror."

Danny must have moved on to another horror movie. Benjy tipped back his chair, listening, his sandwich in one hand, his trumpet balanced on his knees.

The giant ants were trapped in the desert, after having destroyed half of the city of Los Angeles. At a nearby army base jet-fighter pilots were getting ready to bombard them with ant poison. But first they had to get huge tanks of ant poison from the factory, because you can't use a little spray can on a giant ant. The ant poison factory was working overtime to make it all. The giant ants were getting restless in the desert. Would the ant poison get there in time?

"Benjy. Benjy Wilkins! Are you with us today?"

Oh, no. Mr. Maxworthy had finally gotten around to the brass section. Everyone was playing but him, even Danny. And Benjy had a mouth full of peanut butter.

"Yessshh," he managed to get out.

Benjy banged his chair down. His trumpet started to fall. As he grabbed for it, somehow his trumpet collided with his peanut butter sandwich. The sandwich went flying through the air.

"Ta-ta-tum-tum," sang Cynthia Babcock's horn behind him. And then suddenly, "Blaaahpf."

It couldn't be true. But it was. He knew it. Benjy's peanut butter sandwich had landed in her horn.

"Oooh!" shrieked Cynthia. "There's something in my horn. Something disgusting!" She peered inside, trying to find it. Marcia Pendergast, who sat next to her, was trying to help. A kid named Andrew, who sat on the other side, stuck his whole head in. They couldn't find anything. But a very strong smell filled the air. Peanut butter.

"What's going on?" everyone was asking each other. They had all stopped playing. Band period was over anyway. It was time for lunch.

"Mr. Maxworthy, would you please look inside my horn?" Cynthia asked. She sounded like she was about to cry.

"Let's get out of here," Benjy whispered to Danny.

They escaped from the music room fast, before Cynthia Babcock had a chance to put her gifted brain to work on what it was in her horn and how it got there. As soon as they were safely around the corner Danny doubled up laughing. "Hey, that was a good one, Benjy. How'd you ever do it? She'll never get that sandwich out. They'll have to use a hose."

"Even a hose might not do it," said Benjy. "I bet she'll never get rid of the smell. Every time she plays, her horn is going to smell like peanut butter. No one will want to sit next to her." He grinned. It couldn't have happened to a better person—except, of course, Alex Crowley.

Danny smacked himself on the forehead. "That's it!" he said. "*The Brown Slime.* Oh, boy, what a horror movie this could make. First the peanut butter is only in jars and on sandwiches. But then," he lowered his voice ominously, "it spreads."

"Into horns," said Benjy. "Onto people."

"Cars get stuck in it on the freeway, creating the worst traffic jam of the century," Danny went on. "Cows drink from puddles of it and die terrible sticky deaths. It rises higher and higher around the houses, like a flood. And nothing can stop it. Not the police. Not the army. Not even thousands of guys in delicatessens, racing to make it into peanut butter sandwiches. And get this—this movie is brought to you in Smell-o-vision!"

Benjy paused just inside the cafeteria door to drop his lunch bag into the wastebasket. Somehow he seemed to have lost his appetite.

"That," he told Danny, "has got to be the absolute grossest, most disgusting movie ever made."

7

Danny was right. Case the Ace did help the Flannagan team. A whole lot. The next day his three touchdown catches sparked them to a 28–14 win at first recess. At second recess he made one touchdown and a big interception. The Rinaldi team beat them finally, but just barely.

The games were like that all the next week. And the week after too. First the Flannagans would win, and then the Rinaldis. And then it would be tie score. Every game was close. Nobody was trouncing anybody now.

The teams were even, that was for sure. The Rinaldi team had Adam, who was still the best passer.

But Scott and Alex sometimes dropped the ball. The Flannagan team had Case the Ace, who could catch just about anything. But Jason's passes sometimes ended up in the third grade dodge-ball game or in the arms of the other team. The Rinaldi team had Mark Mosquito, who was a fast runner. But sometimes he played soccer. The Flannagan team had Benjy, who was also a fast runner. But sometimes—in fact, most of the time—he got sat on by Alex Crowley.

If only he could figure out a way to get rid of his dumb shadow, Benjy thought, things would be different. Just a few ninety-yard runs would turn things around so the Flannagan team would win every time. And he'd be a star.

He practiced his Billy Joe Crockett moves over and over, before school and after school and sometimes walking down the hall in school. There was a new one he'd seen on TV that was really cool. Billy Joe used it to break out of a tackle. Just when a tackler had his arms wrapped around Billy Joe's legs and it looked like he was going down, he went into a kind of total spin, like a whirling tornado. Tacklers fell over like flies.

Benjy practiced this new move for a whole weekend. On Monday he tried it out in a game.

Spencer and Danny opened up a good hole for him

up the middle. But there was Alex, as usual, right on top of him. Benjy waited until he felt Alex's arms wrap around his shoulders. Then he spun. He could feel Alex's arms losing hold. Benjy twisted away and plunged forward. He got about another ten yards before Adam brought him down.

"Good gain, Benjy," said Jason. "That's playing tough."

He tossed a short pass to Case the Ace, then Kelly took the ball in for the score. The Flannagan team led, 7–0.

But the Rinaldis came right back. Alex caught a long pass and then Mark Mosquito wiggled through a tiny hole in the Flannagan line and then Eddie Spaghetti knocked everyone over to tie the score.

The Flannagan team came roaring back. Benjy took the kickoff and put his best Billy Joe Crockett moves on Mark and Fernando. He got to midfield, to the Rinaldi thirty, the twenty. Then, just as Alex closed in on him, he lateraled to Danny. Only Danny muffed it. He fumbled, right into Scott's hands. Scott tucked the ball under his arm and raced all the way down the field for a touchdown.

The Rinaldis were out in front, 14–7. And recess was almost over. The third-graders were quitting their dodge-ball game.

"Time for one more play," said Jason.

"What's it going to be?" asked Danny, looking worried.

"Fake to Benjy and give it to me," said Kelly.

"Fake to Kelly and give it to me," said Benjy.

"Toss me a long one," said Case the Ace.

"Yeah," said Jason. It was his favorite play. One terrific pass could turn a game around. "Case, go way out. Everyone else block."

Jason stepped up to the line of scrimmage. "Fourteen, thirty-six, ninety-five—hike!"

He faked a handoff to Benjy, then faded back to pass. Case the Ace raced down the field. But the play was not exactly a surprise to the Rinaldi team. Mark and Adam and Scott and Alex and Henry were all chasing him.

Jason waved Case out farther. Benjy and Matthew were blocking Eddie Spaghetti. It was tough work. Keeping Eddie Spaghetti back was like trying to block a ten-ton truck.

Down the field Case the Ace tried desperately to get loose. He zigzagged, losing Adam and Scott. But Mark and Alex stuck right with him.

Jason waved him out still farther. Case faked to the sideline, then cut back to the middle. But still he couldn't shake Mark Mosquito. He was almost to the end zone now.

Jason waved him out once more. What was Jason

doing anyway? He couldn't even throw that far.

Benjy and Matthew couldn't keep Eddie Spaghetti back much longer. He was about to run them over. "Pass it!" Benjy yelled to Jason.

Jason passed it. It wasn't a neat spiral, like Adam always threw, more like a high wobbly fly ball. But it was the longest pass Benjy had ever seen him throw. Either Jason's arm had suddenly gotten powerful, or the ball had been caught by the wind. Case the Ace would never be able to get to it.

Case was in the end zone. He was out of the end zone. He was almost to the woods. He looked back over his shoulder. His long arms reached up. His legs took a giant leap. And then he disappeared.

"Hey," said Danny. "Where did he go?"

"Did he catch it or didn't he?" asked Kelly.

Benjy shaded his eyes and searched down the field. But he couldn't see Case's yellow-and-green football shirt. All he could see was the yellow and green leaves of the woods.

The Flannagan team raced down the field. They peered into the woods.

"Hey, Case! Are you in there?" called Jason.

There was a sudden rustling in the leaves and Case the Ace sat up. "I'm looking for the ball," he said.

"You mean you didn't catch it?" said Kelly.

Case gave her a look as if she were crazy. "In Georgia we don't have to climb trees to catch a pass," he said.

"Sorry about that," said Jason.

"Help me look for the ball," said Case. "It's somewhere in all these red leaves." He started crawling around on his hands and knees.

Benjy and Danny stepped into the woods.

"I'm not going in there," said Jason. "You know what those red leaves are? That's poison ivy."

Benjy stopped short, as if his feet had brakes. He looked at the ground. Jason was right. All those red leaves were in bunches of three. Slowly he backed out of the woods.

Case the Ace stopped looking for the ball. He looked down at the red leaves he was sitting in, the red leaves all around him. "Are you sure?" he asked Jason.

"Sure I'm sure," said Jason. "I've had it about a million times."

"Uh-oh," said Case the Ace very quietly. "I think I'm in big trouble."

Case the Ace was in big trouble. He got poison ivy all over his arms. He got some on his stomach and a lot on his face. He even got some inside his mouth. He must have breathed it in. He was so sick that he had to stay in bed for two days and he couldn't eat. He had to drink through a straw. Finally he came back to school. But he couldn't go out for recess. If he ran around and got hot, it would make his poison ivy itch.

So the Flannagan team didn't have Case the Ace anymore.

Without him, they didn't do so well. They lost to the Rinaldis, 21–7. And 35–14. And 14–0. They tied once. But they didn't win.

A week later, Killer Kelly quit. The soccer teams were having playoffs, and Brian had finally convinced her to play goalie on his team.

"Hey, you can't do that," protested Jason.

Kelly turned around, her hands on her hips. "Why not?" she asked.

"We, uh, need you," said Jason.

"Oh, yeah?" said Kelly. "Well, Brian needs me too. And they have a chance to win, which is more than I can say for this team." And she ran away.

So the Flannagan team didn't have Killer Kelly anymore either.

Without her, they were in big trouble. The Rinaldis trounced them, 42–14. They trampled them, 28–0. They crushed them, 35–7. The games weren't even close anymore. They were a disaster.

Benjy forgot about ninety-yard runs and Billy Joe Crockett moves. He just concentrated on staying alive. He was beginning to feel like one of those old pros who'd been around the NFL a few years. His legs were covered with bruises like polka dots. He counted them in the bathtub one night—twenty-three bright purple bruises. That was probably some kind of NFL record. He didn't get up so fast after one of Alex's tackles now, and when he did sometimes he thought he could hear his bones creaking. One of these days, he thought, he wouldn't get up at all. He'd just lie there, as flat as a potato chip. Crushed once too often by Creepy Crowley.

Something had to be done. Fast.

Jason thought so too. "It's not fair teams anymore," he told Adam. "You've got seven guys and we only have five. Four, if you don't count Matt."

"He counts," said Adam. "He's a body. Anyway, we only have six guys most of the time. Moskowitz would rather play soccer."

Benjy could see why Mark Mosquito might rather play soccer. It probably got boring after a while, winning so much.

"So let's choose new teams," said Jason. "How about it?"

"No way," said Alex, with his nastiest grin. He wasn't bored with winning so much.

"Not a chance," said Scott. "It's class teams, remember?"

"Yeah," said Adam. "You can't change the rules just because you're losing. You better get some new kids on your team."

"Oh, sure," said Jason. "Like who?"

"How about Cynthia Babcock?" snickered Alex. "She's so good at everything, she'd be a star."

"Very funny," said Jason. "Ha, ha, ha."

Benjy wouldn't ask Cynthia Babcock if she was the last person alive on earth. But they had to get somebody.

Jason asked Brian again. He practically fell down on his knees and begged him, but Brian still wouldn't play. "Football is for birdbrains," he said. "Soccer is a game of skill. Watch this." And he dribbled in circles all around Jason.

Benjy asked Todd and Jeff. "Play against those Rinaldi guys?" Todd said. "You must be kidding. I want to live."

"Me too," said Jeff. "If I came home looking like you, Benjy, my mother would kill me."

Benjy looked down at his Cowboys sweat shirt. Every time he took it off, his mother snatched it and washed it. But no matter what kind of soap she used, all the grass stains wouldn't come out. Next to Bad

Bosley Hicks's signature there was a sprinkling of brown spots from the time he got a bloody nose. The shoulder had a hint of spaghetti sauce, and the left sleeve was purple from when he stuck his elbow in Matthew's spilled grape juice. And the white was starting to look gray. Benjy kind of liked it that way, though. It reminded him of how the pros' uniforms looked after a tough game in the rain.

Benjy and Jason carefully examined Case the Ace's spots.

"Hey," said Jason. "They're much better. Really, I can hardly see them at all."

"Yeah," agreed Benjy hopefully. "Practically invisible."

"My mother says I can't go out to recess until the middle of next week," said Case. "She doesn't want to take any chances."

There was only one hope left. Killer Kelly. Maybe they could talk her into coming back to the Flannagan team.

"You ask her," said Benjy. Jason would talk to anybody.

"You ask her," said Jason. Was it possible that even Jason was afraid of her? Yesterday Kelly had told him if he didn't get his foot off her book bag, she would pulverize him.

Benjy studied Kelly from across the classroom. He thought she was looking a little cranky today.

"I know," he whispered to Jason. "Let's write her a note."

"Good idea," Jason whispered back.

It was a good time too. Mr. Flannagan was writing this week's vocabulary words on the blackboard. His back was to the class.

Jason scribbled something on a scrap of notebook paper. He folded it, wrote Kelly's name on it, and passed it to Benjy.

Benjy slipped it to Jennifer. Jennifer tapped Todd on the shoulder. Todd tossed it onto Spencer's desk. Spencer handed it to Kelly.

Kelly unfolded the paper. Even from the back Benjy could see what her answer was going to be. Her ears turned pink. Then she turned around and shook her head.

"That paper doesn't look quite big enough for our long vocabulary words, Kelly. May I see it?"

Mr. Flannagan was standing next to her desk with his hand out.

Uh-oh, thought Benjy. There goes recess.

Kelly handed him the note without a word. She didn't seem so tough with the teacher, Benjy noticed.

Mr. Flannagan walked back to his desk and unfolded the note.

"Jason McFeely," he said. "I see that you feel the need to stay in and study the dictionary during recess today."

"Fifty-two words," said Jason on the bus going home. "Would you believe it? My hand is falling off. I'll never be able to write again." He held out his right hand like a bird with a broken wing.

"Do you think you'll be able to pass again?" Benjy asked.

Jason shrugged. "Who knows? Who cares? Our team has had it. We're all washed up. Defunct."

"Defunct? What's that?"

"All washed up. I got it from the dictionary. I did the D's." Jason tried wiggling his fingers. "No," he said. "Probably I'll never pass again."

"Hey, McFeely!" called a voice from the back of the bus.

Benjy would know that voice anywhere. Alex always sat in the last seat so he could bother people without the bus driver seeing. "It's Creepy Crowley," he said. "Don't turn around."

"What happened to you guys at recess today? Too chicken to play because you know we're going to cream you?"

"Ignore him," Benjy advised. With Alex, it was the only thing to do.

But Jason could never ignore anyone. He turned around in his seat. "I couldn't play," he said. "I got Dictionary."

"Oh, yeah! Sure you did." Alex's voice was closer. He'd moved into the seat right behind them. "You'll probably get it every day now. That way you won't have to play us. Right, McFeely?"

"Wrong, Crowley," said Jason.

"And Benjy-baby." Alex was leaning over the seat now, breathing on them. "He's going to run right home and take his vitamins so he can grow up to be a big running back for the Dallas Cowboys. You better take the whole jar, shrimpo. You've got a long way to go. How can you make the big leagues if you can't even beat us?"

Suddenly Benjy couldn't stand it anymore. He was tired of being sat on by Creepy Crowley. He was tired of having his face rubbed in the dirt. He was tired of listening to his big mouth.

"You think so, huh?" he blurted out. "You really think so? Well, we can beat you guys any old time."

"What did you say, squirt?"

Alex was looking at Benjy as if he couldn't believe his ears. Jason was looking at him as if he were crazy.

"I said we can beat you guys any old time," Benjy

repeated. He felt as if it wasn't him that was doing the talking. He was like a ventriloquist's dummy. Somebody else was making him say these things.

Alex laughed. "Oh, yeah?" he said.

"Yeah," said Benjy.

"Really?"

"Really."

"When?"

"Anytime."

"How about Monday at first recess?" Alex turned around and called to Adam. "Hey, Griffin, get this. Benjy's challenging us to a game. Fourth-grade Super Bowl. He says they can beat us anytime."

Jason nudged Benjy. "At least make it Wednesday," he whispered. "So maybe we'll have Case."

"Wednesday at first recess," said Benjy.

"You guys need all the time you can get," said Alex. "Okay, Wednesday. And just to make it interesting, how about a little bet? I've got a real genuine Dallas Cowboys helmet at home. It'll match your sweat shirt, Benjy-baby. If you beat us, it's yours."

"Okay," said Benjy. He'd seen Alex wearing it a few times. It was pretty cool. Much better than his old beat-up one.

"But if we beat you, I get your sweat shirt to go with my helmet. It's pretty crummy, but I bet it fits me better than it fits you." Alex stuck his hand into Benjy's face. "How about it? Deal?"

Benjy swallowed hard. Then he took Alex's hand and shook it.

"Deal," he said.

8

What was the matter with him? He must be crazy. Absolutely out of his mind. What had ever made him say that the Flannagan team could beat the Rinaldi team any old time, when they couldn't beat them ever? And say it to Alex, of all people. And then he'd made things even worse by making a bet on it. Now he was going to lose his Cowboys sweat shirt on top of everything else. There was no doubt about it—something had gone wrong with his brain.

Jason thought so too. On the bus, after Alex had moved back to laugh with Adam, he'd shaken his head. "Boy, you really told him. You told old Creepy Crowley. But what are you going to do now?"

Benjy didn't know what he was going to do now. He thought the best thing would be to leave town. Go on a long trip and never come back. He never used to understand why kids in books and on TV ran away from home. Now all of a sudden it was perfectly clear.

In his mind he pictured himself packing everything into his knapsack—only how would he fit Clyde?—and hopping a freight train out of town. Or maybe hitchhiking his way out West, with Clyde in one of those little cardboard containers from the Chinese take-out restaurant. The only trouble with these pictures in his mind was that he never saw himself eating. What did the kids who ran away do for food after their fifty-cents-a-week allowance ran out?

Maybe he could go visit his grandmother in Oregon for a while. Like the rest of the year.

He went to try out that idea on his mother. She was sitting at her sewing machine, stitching something small out of black cloth.

"Hey, Mom," he said. "I really miss Grandma Porter. Do you think we could visit her sometime?"

"Sure," said his mother, whirring away at the machine.

"How about tomorrow?"

His mother stopped sewing. She looked at him strangely, like she thought he was crazy too. "You can't go off to Oregon just like that, Benjy," she said. "It's too long a trip. We'll have to plan it for a time like summer, when you have vacation from school."

"Oh," said Benjy. There went that escape.

His mother removed the black cloth from the machine and held it up. "There. How's that for our little witch?"

It was a tiny cape, just Melissa's size. He'd almost forgotten. Halloween was the day after tomorrow.

"Great," said Benjy.

"How about your costume?" asked his mother. "Is it ready?"

"No problem," said Benjy. He was going to be Billy Joe Crockett. His costume was his Cowboys sweat shirt and his helmet. There was nothing to get ready. Except maybe he'd cram some crumpled-up newspapers into his shirt to make his shoulders look bigger.

Thinking about Halloween made Benjy feel a little better. At least he'd have a chance to stuff himself with a few candy bars before he went to his doom next Wednesday.

He went to the phone to call Jason.

"What time are we going out Sunday night?" he asked.

"Hang on," said Jason. "I'll ask my brother."

"What's he got to do with it?" asked Benjy.

"Didn't I tell you?" said Jason. "He said we could come with him. It's going to be so cool. He's got three cans of shaving cream, and his friend Freddy's got these eggs he's been letting get really rotten. It'll be terrific."

"Oh," said Benjy. He had a sudden sinking feeling in his stomach. His mother didn't go for the shaving-cream-and-rotten-eggs part of Halloween. She wasn't going to like this at all.

"He says come over around seven o'clock. Okay?" said Jason.

"Uh, yeah, okay," said Benjy.

But his sinking feeling was right. When he told his mother that they were going with Jason's brother, since he was bigger and could protect them from kids with shaving cream and rotten eggs, she said, "Absolutely not. Those junior-high boys are the ones you need protection *from*. You're not going with them."

"But, Mom," started Benjy.

Her arms were folded. That meant her mind was made up. When his mother's mind was made up, she was like a rock that couldn't be moved no matter what.

He might as well save his energy.

Benjy called Jason back. "My mother won't let me go with your brother," he said. "Can't we just go by ourselves?"

But Jason didn't want to. He'd been trying to get to go with his brother for years. "It's going to be so cool," he kept saying. "You've got to come."

"See you in school Monday," said Benjy.

He called Danny. But Danny was going trick-or-treating with his cousin in the next town. He called Matthew. It would be kind of nice to walk down a dark street with someone as big as him. "Sure," said Matthew. "How many cans of shaving cream do you have? I've got one hidden in my closet and one in my laundry basket."

"Forget it," said Benjy.

He went back to his mother. She was trying the witch costume on Melissa. He had to admit she'd made a good choice. Being a witch suited his sister's personality.

"I've got no one to go trick-or-treating with," he told his mother. "Everyone else is taking shaving cream."

"Well, you'll just have to be the only smart one," she said. "And you do have someone to go with. Your sister."

Benjy had never thought he could sink so low. To have to go trick-or-treating with his baby sister. It was embarrassing. And everyone would know about it too, since his costume wasn't exactly a disguise. If Alex Crowley saw him, he'd die laughing—and draw pictures on his football helmet with shaving cream. He'd be sure to have some. And maybe even Jason would get carried away when he was with his brother and his friends.

There was only one thing to do: find another costume.

Once, a long time ago, before Melissa was born, his mother and father had gone to a Halloween party dressed as Beauty and the Beast. His father had worn a gorilla mask and the furry lining of an old raincoat over his clothes as his costume. They were still around somewhere.

Benjy found them both in the back of the playroom toy closet. He tried them on. The gorilla mask was good. Right away he felt like he was in disguise. And even though it was a little hot, he could breathe and see out the eyes. But the raincoat lining was much too big. He took two steps and fell down.

He went to find his mother. "On second thought," he said, "my costume isn't quite ready. Can you sew this so it fits me?"

On Halloween night Benjy was dressed in his gorilla costume. His mother had sewed the raincoat lining so it fit like his own fur. He thought he looked like King Kong. Melissa was in her witch's costume. She had on a tall pointed hat, some of Benjy's mother's green eye shadow on her cheeks, and she was carrying a little broom from her play cleaning set and a plastic pumpkin. She looked like a fat witch baby.

"I wouldn't want to meet you two on a dark street," Benjy's father said, smiling.

Benjy didn't think he would either. That was good. It meant no one would recognize him. And maybe everyone with shaving cream would stay away from him too.

He beat on his chest like King Kong.

"Now remember, you're only going to the houses on our block," said his mother. "And be sure to hold Melissa's hand. She's never been out after dark before. And if she seems tired or scared, just come home."

"Don't worry, Mom," said Benjy. "I'll take care of her."

It was a perfect Halloween night. There was a moon lurking behind a pile of clouds in a hazy sky. The air was warm. The darkness was full of sounds— faraway giggles, a shriek, running feet. Here and there along the street Benjy could see tiny pinpoints of moving light. Flashlights. He looked for a gang of about six kids that could be Jason, but the block was too quiet.

Benjy took Melissa's hand. She didn't seem a bit scared. She marched along as fast as her fat legs could go, swinging her pumpkin.

Benjy decided to start next door, at Mrs. Rosedale's house.

"When she opens the door," he told Melissa, "say 'Trick or treat.'"

Benjy rang the doorbell. Mrs. Rosedale peered out at them over her silver-rimmed glasses. "Now, who do we have here?" she asked.

"Tick or eat!" said Melissa, her green face beaming.

"Why, I don't believe it!" Mrs. Rosedale beamed back. "It's my little friend from next door. And that must be Benjy in the monkey suit. Why, aren't you just the cutest little witch that ever was! Wait right here, sweetie. I've got something special for you." She went away and came back with a gigantic pumpkin-shaped lollipop. "There you are! And here's one for you too, Benjy. Oh, my, I've never seen anything so precious in all my life. Would you like some Tootsie Rolls too? I suppose you're too young for gum."

"*I'm* not too young for gum," said Benjy.

"No, of course you're not. Here, have some."

Maybe going trick-or-treating with his sister wasn't so bad, after all, Benjy thought, if this was how it was going to be.

And it was. At every house they went to the grown-ups carried on as if they'd never seen a baby before.

They pinched Melissa's cheeks. They said she was the sweetest thing. They called other people to come to the door and look. At one house, the Fryhoffers' across the road, they even took pictures of her.

And they loaded her up with candy. Since Benjy was with her, they loaded him up too. By the time he'd finished all the houses on his block, his shopping bag was almost half full. And he'd taken the biggest one his mother had. Melissa's pumpkin was over-flowing. It was too heavy for her to carry, so Benjy had to carry the treats for both of them. Plus the flashlight. Plus he had to keep picking up her broom.

It was time to go home. But Benjy hated to stop. He was getting so much good stuff. Maybe he could fill his bag all the way to the top. And he could tell Melissa didn't want to go home. She was having the time of her life. She kept cramming candy into her mouth and saying, "Tick or eat! Tick or eat!"

He decided to go to one more house. The Ma-honeys, on the next corner, always had a terrific Halloween display in their yard—tombstones and dancing skeletons and stuff like that. He went there every year. His mother wouldn't mind if he took Melissa, since she wasn't tired or scared. They would just go there, and maybe a couple of houses along the way, and then go home.

"Come on, Melissa," he said. "Let's go get some more candy."

She trotted happily along next to him.

They passed a clown and a ballerina, walking with a father wearing a werewolf mask.

"Greetings, King Kong," said the werewolf.

"Doggie?" said Melissa.

They saw a ghost, a princess, and a white rabbit.

"Kitty-cat?" said Melissa.

She was really confused. But it was too hard to explain, Benjy decided. He was a little confused himself. Who were the ghost and the white rabbit? Why hadn't he seen anyone he knew? Where was Jason? And Alex?

All of a sudden feet came pounding down the driveway of the Schaefers' house. "Got you!" "Did not!" "Oh, yeah? You better run!" A gang of tramps came racing toward them. They had blackened faces and shirttails sticking out and they were all carrying shaving cream cans. One of them had to be Jason.

Benjy started to say "Hey, Jason!" But then he changed his mind. He waited to see if Jason would recognize him.

"Hey, you guys!" yelled one tramp in a high top hat. Benjy thought it was Jason's brother, but he wasn't sure. "Let's go down Mayberry."

Jason was standing practically next to Benjy. He looked a wreck. His father's old sport jacket was covered with white blobs of shaving cream. And there was a smell of rotten eggs in the air.

For a second he looked right at Benjy. Then the tramp with the high hat said, "Come on!" And Jason ran off down the street.

Benjy couldn't believe it. Even Jason didn't know him. His gorilla costume really was a disguise. And he hadn't noticed Melissa. Benjy felt terrific all of a sudden, like he had some secret power. Somehow, in the darkness, this wasn't the street he walked down every day, and inside his gorilla suit this wasn't really him.

"Eee-yah!" he yelled, beating on his chest.

The corner of White Oak looked like a convention of flashlights. The Mahoneys had really outdone themselves this year. The front yard had about six tombstones, with black cats and skulls sitting on top of them. A man appeared to be falling out of an upstairs window. From somewhere inside there were sounds of creaking doors and moans and every once in a while a terrible scream. In the middle of the lawn stood three witches, stirring up something in a huge black pot.

Benjy knew how they did it, with timers and motors and records playing inside the house. But still he felt a shiver run up his spine. Those witches sure looked real.

He looked down to see how Melissa was taking it. She was staring at the witches with eyes as round as pancakes. Uh-oh. Maybe she was going to start screaming. He shouldn't have brought her. She was too little.

"Itch!" she cried, laughing.

She thought they were big versions of herself. She ran toward the three witches. If Benjy hadn't grabbed her, she would have fallen into the pot. Inside, he saw, there was no toad soup, but a spotlight and a motor that made the witches look like they were stirring. They really were dummies.

Melissa struggled out of his arms. She ran over to one of the tombstones. "Kitty-cat!" she crowed. Then she ran to another. "Da-da!" Did she think the skull was her father? It didn't matter. She was having a great time. When one of the Mahoney boys dressed as a skeleton jumped out from behind a bush and yelled "Boo!" she yelled "Boo!" back. And when she saw Mrs. Mahoney, dressed up as a witch, handing out treats at the front door, Benjy thought she'd go crazy. "Itch! Itch!" she shouted, hugging Mrs. Mahoney's leg. Probably she'd never let go. Probably they'd have to stay there all night.

While Benjy was waiting for her to wear herself

out, he looked around the yard. There sure were a lot of kids. Everyone came to the Mahoneys' on Halloween. He tried to figure out who was who under their costumes. That little spaceman over there was Adam Bolton from down the street, he bet. He was always playing space games. And the even littler robot was his brother, Jeremy. Yes, there was Mrs. Bolton sitting in her car waiting for them. Was it possible that those two ladies in the evening dresses and high heels over there were Cynthia Babcock and her friend Gretchen the Pain? It had to be. Only one girl in the world had hair like Gretchen the Pain. And how about those two kids hanging around the Mahoneys' mailbox down by the road? One was wearing a devil mask and the other one was some sort of deformed monster. The monster's face wasn't familiar, but his red plaid shirt was. Where had Benjy seen it before?

The devil and the monster were whispering and nudging each other. They circled the mailbox. Suddenly they stuffed something inside. Then they took off down the road so fast it looked like a ghost was chasing them.

Now Benjy knew where he'd seen the red plaid shirt before. It was the shirt Alex Crowley had worn to school on Friday. And the kid inside the devil mask must be Brian. Of course, those two wouldn't let Halloween go by without making trouble.

"Yi-yi-*yow*!"

There was a big commotion by the Mahoneys' front door. A kid was jumping up and down, holding on to his leg. Mrs. Mahoney put down her basket of treats to see what was wrong. A boy in a Frankenstein outfit was yelling, "She did it!"

Benjy had the terrible feeling that he knew who "she" was.

He looked again at the boy who was jumping up and down. He had on a weird costume. He was dressed as a chocolate chip cookie.

Oh, no! How dumb could his sister be? She must have taken a bite out of him.

He found Melissa standing next to Mrs. Mahoney's basket, helping herself to a few more lollipops. He grabbed her. "We've got to get out of here," he said.

She didn't protest. Maybe even she had had enough candy. Or maybe she was finally getting tired.

Benjy didn't let go of Melissa's hand all the way home. They didn't stop at any more houses. He didn't care if his bag was full to the top. He didn't like to eat too much of that junk anyway.

They were almost to their house when Benjy noticed a shadow moving in the darkness ahead of them. A figure separated itself from a tree trunk and moved toward Mrs. Rosedale's mailbox. And then another one. Alex and Brian—it had to be.

The shadows opened her mailbox and put something inside. Now they were moving to the next one. Benjy's mailbox.

Inside his gorilla suit Benjy felt his face getting hot. Those guys weren't going to mess up his mailbox. Not with King Kong around. He felt himself swelling inside, growing bigger. Like the real King Kong.

"Eee-yah!" he cried.

The shadows at the mailbox turned around. It was them, all right. Benjy could see the scar across the deformed monster's face.

He reached inside his sister's pumpkin for something to throw. Right on top was an egg. Where in the world had she picked that up?

He heaved it toward the mailbox.

"Yowp!"

He couldn't believe it. He'd scored a direct hit. Right in the middle of Alex's red plaid shirt.

He reached in again. Another egg. Boy, was she good at providing ammunition. This one zipped by Brian's ear and landed in the bushes. A rotten smell filled the air.

"Me!" cried Melissa, laughing. She started grabbing things from the pumpkin and throwing them— candy bars, apples, lollipops. An apple got Alex in the rear end. She had some arm for a one-and-a-half-year-old kid.

Now they had them on the run.

"Eee-yah!" yelled Benjy, beating on his chest and stamping his feet. Melissa lifted up her broom and started chasing them.

Alex and Brian took off down the road as if a hundred ghosts were after them.

"Eee-yah! Eee-yah!"

"Tick or eat! Tick or eat!"

They disappeared into the darkness.

Inside his gorilla mask Benjy started to laugh. He laughed until he nearly fell down in the road.

Going trick-or-treating with his sister hadn't been so bad after all.

9

Something was wrong with Benjy's hair. It had gotten long and curly. His hair had never been curly before. It stood up all over his head, sort of like King Kong. How come his mother hadn't taken him to the barber shop? She always dragged him down there the minute it started to look good. Benjy had so much hair that he couldn't get on his football helmet. He tugged at it. He tried to mash his hair down. He tried stretching the helmet. But it was no use. His hair was too big for his helmet. He couldn't play football.

Benjy woke up sweating, his stomach tied in a knot. He reached up and touched his hair. It felt flat, just like normal. Thank goodness—it had only been a dumb dream.

But he still felt twitchy inside. The game. The fourth-grade Super Bowl. It was on Wednesday, and this was already Monday. He had to figure out a way to win and show old Creepy Crowley. But how? Things didn't look too good for the good guys.

When Benjy finally went back to sleep, he dreamed that a train was bearing down on him, tooting and puffing black smoke. He couldn't get out of the way. It was like his feet were stuck to the ground. And leaning out of the train window, waving, was this deformed monster in a red plaid shirt.

At breakfast Benjy talked to his father.

"Uh, Dad," he said. "What would you do if there was a game you had to win, but all the guys on the other team were bigger and stronger and there were more of them than there were of you?"

"What kind of game?" Benjy's father asked, slowly spreading strawberry jam on his toast.

"Football," said Benjy. "At recess."

"I'd stay in for recess," said his father.

"Dad!" said Benjy, shocked. Some help he was.

"Well, I was always kind of small for my age," his father explained. "And if there was one thing I hated, it was ending up underneath a pile of bigger kids. There was this one kid I remember who liked to see if he could rub my nose in the dirt. Michael Murphy, his name was. A really terrific kid."

It was strange, Benjy thought, that even though a lot of things had changed from long ago when his father was a boy, some things hadn't changed.

"But I can't stay in for recess," Benjy said. Alex would never let him hear the end of that. "I have to play. And we have to win. It's very important."

"Hmmm," said his father. "Let me think about it."

He chewed on his toast. He ate an entire scrambled egg and wiped up his plate with a triangle of toast. He drained his coffee cup. Then he leaned toward Benjy. "Use this," he said, tapping his forehead. "Brains beat brawn anytime. Surprise them."

He pushed back his chair. "Got to go now. I'm late. Good luck, Benjy." He ruffled Benjy's flat hair and left the table.

Benjy thought about what his father had said. It sounded good, only he wasn't exactly sure what it meant. Surprise them. What could the Flannagan team possibly do that would surprise the Rinaldi team? They'd already tried everything.

During library period at school, Benjy sat on the floor in front of the 796.33 shelf and read all the football books he could find. *Great Running Backs of Football History. Super Bowl Spotlight. Heroes of the NFL Today.*

Somehow there weren't any surprises in any of them. The way the writers of the books seemed to see it, winning was easy. All you had to do was hand off the ball to a hero of the NFL and seconds later . . . touchdown! A hero of the NFL couldn't be stopped. But what did you do if you didn't happen to have a hero of the NFL handy?

Benjy checked out three of the books, but he didn't have too much hope.

He talked to Jason.

"Case thinks he'll be able to play by Wednesday, but he's not sure," said Jason. "His mother is still afraid if he moves, his spots are going to spread. There's one good thing about poison ivy, though. He hasn't taken a bath in eight days."

"What about Kelly?" Benjy asked.

Jason shook his head glumly. "I asked Jennifer to ask her. No luck."

Probably Case couldn't play and Kelly wouldn't play and it was just going to be the five of them against the Rinaldi team. Four, really, because no matter what Adam said, you couldn't count Matthew. And Benjy couldn't think of a single surprise they could pull. Things looked pretty bleak for the good guys.

"So what do we do now?" Benjy asked.

"One thing we could do," said Jason, "is practice."

It seemed like a good idea. They had to do something.

"My house after school?" said Benjy. His yard was better than Jason's for football. Jason lived on a hill. Jason nodded. "I'll tell the other guys."

At three thirty that afternoon Benjy was in his front yard, waiting for Jason and Danny and Spencer and Matthew. Their mothers were going to drive them over as soon as they got home from school.

Benjy was practicing his Billy Joe Crockett moves while he waited. Maybe there was something he wasn't doing quite right. Maybe if he changed one little thing—like the way he pointed his shoulders or something—he'd be able to break away from Alex and go all the way for a touchdown.

He noticed Charlie Fryhoffer's car, a souped-up purple Volkswagen, zip around the corner and into his driveway. Charlie Fryhoffer lived across the street. Now he worked in a gas station, but a couple of years ago he'd been a football star at the high school. Benjy forgot what position he'd played. A couple of years ago he hadn't been interested in football.

Benjy wandered across the street, tossing his football from one hand to the other. Charlie Fryhoffer was washing his car in the driveway. His car was the big thing in his life. All the time he wasn't working or driving around in it he was washing it.

"Hi," said Benjy. He thought he'd show Charlie

how he could spin a perfect spiral. But the ball got away from him and spun right into Charlie's bucket. Water splashed on his feet. "Sorry," said Benjy.

"That's okay," said Charlie. "How're you doing?"

"Fine," said Benjy.

Charlie didn't say anything else. He wasn't much of a talker. Frowning, he rubbed at a spot on his fender that Benjy couldn't even see.

"Uh, I was wondering," Benjy began. He wasn't sure exactly what he wanted to ask. Something about getting to be a football star. "Uh, do you have any tips about football you can give me? Like what I should practice and things like that?"

Charlie Fryhoffer stopped working on the invisible spot. He stared at Benjy. "You want to be a football player?" he said, as if he found it hard to believe.

Benjy nodded.

Charlie looked him over from top to bottom. "How much do you weigh?" he asked.

"Uh, sixty-two." That was with his sneakers on and his Cowboys sweat shirt and his helmet.

Charlie stood up. All of a sudden Benjy remembered what position he'd played in high school. Tackle. He must weigh 200 pounds. Maybe 250. He was almost as big as Bad Bosley Hicks.

Slowly he shook his head. "I'd forget it if I were you," he said.

"But I'm going to grow," Benjy protested. "I'll get heavier. I eat a lot. I'm always eating."

"Sure you will," said Charlie. "Still, I'd go out for soccer. Or baseball."

So that was it. His football career was over. Finished before it even got off the ground. He'd never be a hero of the NFL, at least if he listened to Charlie Fryhoffer.

Charlie knelt down again and started polishing his fender with a funny-looking blue cloth.

"Can I ask you one more question?" said Benjy. He saw Danny's car turning into his own driveway.

"Sure," said Charlie.

"How can you win a game when the other team has more players and they're pretty much bigger and better than you are?"

Charlie gave it some thought while he polished the fender until Benjy could see his face in it.

Finally he said, "I'd say probably you can't."

This guy was a real ray of sunshine.

"Thanks a lot," said Benjy. And he went back across the street to meet Danny.

Jason practiced throwing long bombs to Spencer. He was looking good, Benjy thought, as Spencer made five easy catches in a row. Maybe Jason was going to turn out to have the powerful, accurate arm of Johnny

Hopkins, the Cowboys quarterback. Then Jason threw one that sailed about a mile over Spencer's head and disappeared into the branches of the maple tree by the driveway. Jason had to climb the tree to get it. He wasn't quite Johnny Hopkins yet, Benjy decided.

Benjy and Danny practiced their running game. Benjy showed Danny some of his Billy Joe Crockett moves. Danny faked to the outside, cut to the inside, slipped, and fell down. No gain.

Then Benjy and Danny practiced some passing while Jason and Spencer did a little running. That might be a surprise to the Rinaldi team, Benjy thought. Only neither Benjy nor Danny could throw the ball as far as Jason could. And Spencer was too slow a runner. And Jason was too easy to tackle.

"Can I try carrying the ball?" asked Matthew.

Benjy looked at him. A turtle with a broken leg could run faster than Matthew could. But he looked so hopeful. They might as well try it. They'd tried everything else.

Spencer snapped the ball to Jason. Jason handed off to Matthew. Matthew took one step and Benjy tackled him.

Only he wouldn't go down. Danny tackled him from the other side. Matthew staggered a little, but he kept going. Spencer dove for his legs. Matthew

kept on moving, dragging Benjy and Danny and Spencer with him.

Jason jumped on his back. Finally Matthew went down.

But he went down on Benjy's foot.

"Yow!" cried Benjy.

He was on the bottom of a pile of guys, being smothered by Matthew, who weighed a ton, and his right foot hurt like crazy.

Everyone piled off. Matthew helped Benjy up. "Sorry I stepped on you," he said. "Are you okay?"

Benjy wiggled his foot. Pain darted through it. He tried to take a step. Pain shot through it like an arrow.

He sat down again. "No," he said.

This was all he needed. Probably his foot was broken. Probably he wouldn't even be able to play in the fourth-grade Super Bowl. And Alex Crowley would say he'd broken his foot on purpose because he was too chicken to play.

Things looked totally terrible for the good guys.

10

It turned out that Benjy didn't have a broken foot. It was just bruised—the biggest, darkest, purplest bruise in his whole collection of bruises. He would be able to play in the fourth-grade Super Bowl. The thing he wouldn't be able to do was run fast and score touchdowns.

In some ways Benjy thought he would have preferred being on crutches.

His mother suggested that soaking his foot in water might help. So Benjy sat with it in a pan of water, watching *Monday Night Football* on TV. The Cowboys were playing the Seahawks. And of course, the Cowboys were going to win. The Seahawks were terrible. They'd only won two games this season. But this was Benjy's chance to study Billy Joe Crockett and his great moves one more time.

As always, Billy Joe was terrific. He slipped through the smallest holes in the Seahawks line. He completely changed direction in the middle of a step to fake out a tackler, then turned on the speed and galloped down the sidelines. And when someone finally got his hands on him, he somehow managed to slip away, as if his uniform were greased, and pick up an extra five yards before three or four guys brought him down.

Benjy watched, wiggling his foot in his pan of water, and then checking to see how much it hurt. It hurt a lot. His foot seemed a little swollen too, or maybe it just looked that way because he was seeing it through water. One thing was sure—he wasn't going to be able to use any of these great moves in his game.

With Billy Joe Crockett's running and Johnny Hopkins's passing, the Cowboys got off to a 14–0 lead. This game was in their pocket.

"The Cowboys offense looks awesome in the first quarter," the announcer told everyone.

Finally the Seahawks had the ball. Benjy wasn't worried. They would never be able to do anything against the tough Cowboys defense.

But on the very first play the Seahawks quarterback pulled a surprise move. He handed off to the half-back, who started running to the right side. He didn't get very far against the tough Cowboys defense. But then, just as he was about to be tackled, the halfback threw the ball. It was a long pass—and it was caught on the Cowboys ten yard line. The Cowboys were stunned, said the announcer, and it looked like he was right because on the very next play a Seahawks runner shot into the end zone without the Cowboys getting a hand on him.

"The extra point is good. It's fourteen to seven, and the Seahawks are right back in this ball game!" the announcer said, sounding excited. He hadn't been that excited when the Cowboys scored, Benjy thought. Probably he was secretly a Seahawks fan.

It was just a lucky break. The Seahawks couldn't do that again, not against the Cowboys. But the next time the Seahawks got the ball after the Cowboys full-back fumbled, they did do it again. One runner started around left end, taking all the Cowboys de-fense with him. Then he lateraled to another guy, who ran the other way. Nobody was on that side of the field, and he had an easy gain of twenty-two yards.

The Seahawks used funny formations too. Some-thing called an "R-formation," a six-man line, a four-man line, a floating wide receiver. "I've never seen a two-man line before," the announcer exclaimed at one point, sounding as if he were falling out of his chair. Sometimes they took a long time in the huddle, and sometimes they didn't go into a huddle at all. It was supposed to mix up the defense.

And it was working. The Cowboys didn't know what was going to happen next. When the Seahawks lined up for a field goal on the thirty, and somehow the quarterback ended up catching a pass and running it in for a touchdown, even the announcer sounded confused.

"That's a new one on me," he said. "I guess we could call it a fake field goal quarterback option play. Or a fake option quarterback field goal play. Or something. But one thing is clear. Bart Thorn, the Seahawks quarterback, is calling a brilliant game here today."

For the first time Benjy really took a good look at Bart Thorn. He was kind of a small, skinny guy, at least compared to all those huge tackles and line-backers and running backs who were pounding him on the back on the sidelines. But he was using his brain to confuse the Cowboys and maybe to beat them. That was what his father had been talking about at breakfast, Benjy realized. That was what he meant by "Surprise them."

And suddenly Benjy knew what the Flannagan team was going to have to do to beat the Rinaldi team in the fourth-grade Super Bowl.

The score was all tied up now, 14–14, and the Seahawks were kicking off to the Cowboys. Now was the time the Cowboys could use some fancy running by Billy Joe Crockett.

"Benjy!" called his mother down the stairs. "Bedtime."

"Can I just watch till halftime? Please?" Benjy said. "It's only eight minutes."

But his mother knew that eight minutes of football wasn't the same as eight regular minutes.

"Now," she said in her you-can't-change-my-mind-I'm-a-rock-that-can't-be-moved voice.

"Oh, okay," grumbled Benjy. But actually he didn't mind so much turning it off. His brain was buzzing with fake field goals and passing halfbacks and receiving quarterbacks and weird formations. He needed to make plans.

As Benjy lay in bed, staring up at the ceiling, the plays they would use popped into his head like he was looking at them on a giant TV screen.

There was Spencer running to the right, then suddenly tossing a pass to Case the Ace, who had sneaked down the field when no one was looking. And Danny running around left end into a wall of tacklers, then suddenly lateraling to Benjy, who ran the other way, all the way for a score. Wait—he'd better change that because of his foot. Make it Benjy lateraling to Danny. Or how about a double lateral play? If Kelly would only stop playing soccer and come back, that one could be beautiful. And they could pull a fake field goal quarterback option play, or whatever it was called, even though they didn't have field goals because they didn't have goal posts. They'd switch quarterbacks suddenly, with Benjy taking the snap and Jason going out for a pass. The Rinaldi team wouldn't know who had the ball. Old Creepy Crowley would be so mixed up, he wouldn't know who to tackle.

Benjy turned on his flashlight and drew diagrams of his plays, using little *X*'s and *O*'s like they did on TV, so he could show Jason tomorrow. Boy, was he going to be surprised.

And then one more play popped into Benjy's head. It was the one they'd tried this afternoon, the one where Matthew carried the ball. If anything would surprise the Rinaldi team, that play would do it. Who cared that Matthew couldn't run as fast as a turtle with a broken leg? The big thing was that no one could get him down. It had taken four of them to tackle him today, and while they were trying he'd dragged them ten yards, at least. That could be enough for a touchdown.

Yes, thought Benjy, drawing in a few more *X*'s on top of the big *O* that was Matthew. This might just turn out to be the game-winning play.

And better still, maybe Matthew would step on Alex's foot.

11

"Did you see the Cowboys–Seahawks game last night?" asked Jason on the bus the next morning.

"Part of it," said Benjy. Jason's mother didn't make him go to bed before halftime, he knew. She was so busy worrying about his older sister driving the car and his older brother wrecking the furniture practicing weightlifting that she didn't even notice what Jason did. It must be nice to be the youngest. "Who won, anyway?"

"Cowboys in overtime, thirty-four to thirty-one. What a game! That Bart Thorn was okay. But Carlisle kicked a field goal with eight seconds left. Did you see Billy Joe Crockett's seventy-six-yard run in the first quarter? Wasn't that amazing?"

Benjy nodded. But for once he didn't feel like talking about Billy Joe Crockett. He took out his pages with the X's and O's and showed them to Jason.

"What's all this stuff?" asked Jason.

"A few Bart Thorn plays," said Benjy. He showed Jason the halfback pass play and the double lateral play and the Matthew-carries-the-ball play.

Jason started nodding his head. By the time Benjy got to the quarterback-catches-a-pass play he was grinning.

"You know, Benjy," he said, "we might just possibly have a chance."

All the rest of the day at school Jason drew little X's and O's in the margins of his English homework and his math paper and his vocabulary test. Once, when Mr. Flannagan wasn't looking, he passed one to Benjy. Benjy couldn't figure out what it was all about. He'd never seen so many arrows pointing every which way. He raised his eyebrows at Jason.

"Hidden ball trick," whispered Jason.

Benjy hoped Jason knew what he was doing.

On the way to music class Jason whispered to Case the Ace.

"He's definitely playing," he reported to Benjy. "No matter what his mother says."

During lunch Jason whispered to Jennifer, who whispered to Kelly.

"She might and she might not," Jason told Benjy.

That sounded a little bit hopeful. And then after lunch, when Jason mentioned that he was working on a terrific play where Kelly would definitely score a touchdown, Jennifer whispered, "She might not and she might."

She was going to play, Benjy thought. She just wanted to make Jason suffer as long as possible.

At recess all of the Flannagan team sat on the edge of the sandbox where the kindergarten kids played, and studied the pages with the X's and O's. By now there were a lot of pages. Benjy and Jason called them their playbook.

Case the Ace liked the halfback pass play. Danny liked the hidden ball trick. "I could carry it under my shirt," he suggested. But Jason thought that was illegal. "We can't afford any penalties," he said.

Matthew, of course, liked the play where he carried the ball. In fact, he liked it so much he kept repeating "Oh, boy, I get to carry the ball!" over and over. His round face beamed as bright as the sun coming out.

"Ssshh," said Benjy and Jason together, looking around for spies. But no one was there. The Rinaldi team was practicing whipping them down on the lower field.

At second recess the Flannagan team went out behind the oak tree, past the second-grade kickball game, far from the lower field, and practiced handing off, lateraling, and hiding the ball. They did it until they could do it all without a fumble.

On the way home on the bus Benjy and Jason sat slouched down in a seat, studying their playbook hidden inside Jason's social studies book. They'd given the plays code numbers.

"We'll definitely use twenty-two-X," said Jason. "And forty-seven-T is going to kill them!"

"Don't forget fifty-seven-J," said Benjy. That was the hidden ball trick.

"Yeah," said Jason. "Boy, oh, boy, that's going to be so cool. I'd like to take a picture of old Creepy Crowley's face when we pull that one."

And on the way off the bus, he just happened accidentally to bump into old Creepy Crowley.

Alex glared at him. But then his glare turned into a grin. "Hey, McFeely," he said. "You guys ready for the big game tomorrow?"

Jason grinned back. "As a matter of fact," he said, "I think we are."

Benjy went to bed early that night. First he gave his foot another soak. He didn't really think it was helping, but he figured that was what the trainer would make him do if he was in the NFL. Then he laid out his clothes on his chair. His lucky sneakers that he'd made a homerun in kickball in, his old jeans with the patched knees, and of course his wristbands and his Cowboys sweat shirt. Then he got into bed. He put his playbook under his pillow, in case maybe someone might try to steal it. Also in case great play ideas might trickle into his mind while he was sleeping.

Maybe it was the playbook under his pillow, but he had weird dreams all night. One had something to do with flying and the Goodyear blimp. In another one he was playing football in a huge stadium full of yelling people. He was wearing a brand-new blue-and-white uniform that fit just right. He seemed to be the Cowboys quarterback, and this was the Super Bowl. The only thing was that he couldn't hang on to the football. Balls were flying through the air, but they were all just out of his reach. Every time he thought he had one it would squirt out of his hands and go sailing into the stands. There were footballs all over the place, but none for him.

When he got out of bed in the morning, Benjy checked out his foot. The purple was fading to an interesting blue-yellow color, but it still hurt when he wiggled it. He wasn't going to have his full running speed, that was for sure. He got dressed and stuffed his playbook in his back pocket. "Well, Clyde, old buddy," he said, "wish me luck."

Clyde opened and closed his mouth. He could have been saying "Good luck," or he could just have been chewing. You could never tell with a goldfish. It was nice in a way that Clyde never got excited. It made it seem as if all the things there were to worry about weren't worth worrying about. On the other hand, sometimes Benjy thought that Clyde just didn't care.

"So long, pal," he said.

Breakfast was a problem. Benjy didn't know whether to stuff himself and be full of strength and energy but maybe be weighed down by so much food, or take it easy and be light and fast but maybe be weak. NFL players always had steak and eggs before a game, he thought. Or was that boxers? Or astronauts?

It didn't really matter. His mother would never fix him a steak for breakfast anyway. He had the egg part and juice and a doughnut and a small bowl of Zingies. It was a lot, but not too much.

"So," said his father, "today's the big day."

How did his father always seem to know things without asking? Was it Benjy's clothes, or maybe the way he was eating? Benjy looked at his hand holding a spoonful of Zingies. At least it wasn't shaking.

"Do you think you'll win?"

"Maybe," said Benjy.

Benjy's father pointed to his forehead. "Remember," he said, smiling. "And good luck."

Good luck was something they really could use.

First recess was at 10:45. The clock in their room was never going to get that far at the rate it was going. 9:10, 9:13, 9:17. A half hour later it was only 9:26. Benjy tried to listen to Mr. Flannagan talking about the human body and the way blood traveled through the tentacles to the heart, or something like that. But his mind kept wandering. He went over play 22-X in his mind. He stared at the back of Kelly's head and wondered if she still could run. She was definitely playing. Jennifer had whispered it to Jason getting off the school bus.

Jason's mind was wandering too. Benjy could tell. He kept drawing little *X*'s and *O*'s on the cover of his social studies book and then erasing them. He got up to sharpen his pencil. Then he went to the boys' room.

When Jason came back, he had a funny look on his face. Like he was trying not to laugh but was having a tough time keeping it in. What was going on? Had he thought up a game-winning play in the boys' room?

The minute Mr. Flannagan turned around to write on the blackboard, a note landed on Benjy's desk. "Go to the boys' room," it said.

Benjy looked over at Jason. He was nodding and jerking his head toward the boys' room. This must be important.

Benjy raised his hand and got permission to go. In the boys' room he closed the door and looked around. Now what? Had Jason left a message for him or something? Nothing looked any different. The boys' room, which was only big enough for one person, was as messy as usual. Soap was in the sink and paper towels on the floor.

There was a tap on the door. "It's me," said Jason's voice.

Benjy let him in. "What's going on, anyway?" he asked. Usually Mr. Flannagan only let one boy go to the boys' room at a time.

"I told him I felt sick," Jason said. He locked the door. His face fell apart into a total grin. "It's happened!" he said. "Finally, after all these years."

"What's happened?" Somehow this didn't sound like a game-winning play.

Jason pointed to the wall above the sink, way up close to the ceiling.

Benjy didn't see anything.

"Where?"

"There," said Jason. "Don't you see it? A hole."

There was a little hole in the plaster, next to a pipe.

"So?" said Benjy. He still didn't get it.

"So we can look through. Into the girls' room."

For two years Jason had been talking about how cool it would be if they could spy on the girls in the girls' room next door. But Benjy had never thought it would really happen. Maybe Jason had made the hole himself. But he couldn't have. It was up too high. In fact, it was up too high to look through.

Not for Jason, though. "What are we waiting for?" he said. "I've got to try this."

Jason put one foot on the toilet seat. Then, grabbing hold of the metal paper towel machine, he pulled himself up on the sink. "Hold on to my legs," he told Benjy. He clutched at the wall. His eyes came to just below the hole. "If only I was as tall as my brother," he muttered. He stood on his tiptoes, stretching as high as he could. "I can see!" he whispered. "Hey, it works!" He wiggled around, trying to get the best view. "Don't let go of my ankles, Benjy, whatever you do."

Benjy heard a noise outside. "I think someone's going in," he said.

Jason craned his neck so hard he looked like some kind of long-necked bird. "I can see her!" he whispered. "Oh, boy, it's Cynthia. Old Big Brains Babcock!"

Benjy thought Jason was going to fall off the sink, he was so excited. He held tight to his ankles.

"She's washing her hands," Jason reported. A minute later he said, "She's drying her hands. Is that all she's going to do?" He sounded disappointed.

"Now what?" asked Benjy.

"Uh, let's see. She's getting something out of her schoolbag. It's a comb. Now she's combing her hair. Still combing. Got a few tangles there."

"Can I see?" asked Benjy.

"Sure," said Jason. "Looks like those tangles are going to take awhile."

He jumped down. Benjy climbed up carefully and stretched until he could look through the hole. "All I can see is the ceiling," he said.

"You've got to move around a little," said Jason. "Don't worry. I've got your ankles."

Suddenly the mirror came into view. And there was old Cynthia, looking at herself in it. She was putting barrettes in her hair now, dumb-looking pink ones with purple hearts.

"What's she up to now?" whispered Jason. "Anything good?"

"Still working on her hair," reported Benjy.

"Putting barrettes in. Taking them out. Trying a different hairstyle. Hey, now she's doing all kinds of weird poses in front of the mirror, smiling at herself. She really thinks she's hot stuff."

"I've got it!" said Jason, letting go of Benjy's ankles.

"What's the idea?" protested Benjy.

"I'm going to send her a note," said Jason. He ripped off a piece of paper towel. "How's this? 'Mirror, mirror on the wall, who's the weirdest-looking one of all?' "

"You can't do that," said Benjy. "She'll know we're spying."

"We've got to do it. Oh, it'll be so cool! She'll keel over. Let me up there. I'm going to do it."

You couldn't argue with Jason when he had a hot idea.

Benjy got himself down and boosted Jason up. Jason rolled up the note into a skinny wad and pushed it through the hole.

"It landed behind her," he said. "She's turning around. She's bending over." He craned his neck farther to see. "She's —"

Suddenly Jason was thrashing his arms, struggling to get his balance. He snatched at the wall, the top of the mirror. Benjy tried to hold on to his legs, but his left foot slipped off the sink. Jason made a desperate grab for the paper towel machine. Paper towels started falling out. It was raining paper towels. And then the machine came off the wall. Benjy ducked under the sink as Jason and all the paper towels and the paper towel machine came crashing to the floor.

For a minute nothing happened. Benjy and Jason looked at each other. "You all right?" asked Jason, lying flat on a bed of paper towels next to the toilet.

Benjy sat up under the sink, rubbing his elbow. "I think so. You?"

"I have no idea," said Jason.

And then there was pounding on the door, and Mr. Flannagan's voice. "Jason? Benjy! Open the door."

Slowly Benjy got up and went to the door.

"What's going on here? What was that noise? Are you all right?"

The whole class was standing outside, peering in.

"Stand back and give them room," Mr. Flannagan said, frowning. He looked as if he wasn't really sure whether to be angry or worried. "What in the world happened to you boys? It sounded like an earthquake, at least."

Jason got to his feet, checking out each part of his body for damage. Nothing seemed to be broken, anyway. "Well, uh, it was the paper towel machine," he said. "All of a sudden, it just fell off the wall. And we were standing there, and it knocked us over."

"The paper towel machine," repeated Mr. Flannagan. "Just fell off the wall. Just like that. No earthquake or anything." His sharp eyes looked from
Jason to Benjy to the paper towel machine.

Benjy and Jason both nodded, looking down at the
floor.

"I bet that's not how it really happened," said Cynthia Babcock, pushing through to the front of the
class. Her hair was pinned up in a really funny way,
Benjy noticed. And in her hand was a little rolled-up
wad of paper towel.

All of a sudden a terrible picture flashed into Benjy's
mind. It was a picture of *Webster's Unabridged Dictionary*. The one on Mr. Flannagan's desk. The one
with all the words in the English language inside of it.

12

The fourth-grade Super Bowl was postponed. "Postponed on account of Dictionary," Jason told everyone. He and Benjy had to stay in for both recesses. They each copied half a page. That was eighty-six words altogether. The *M*'s this time. *Monotonous* was the word for copying from the dictionary. *Merciless* was the word for Mr. Flannagan.

While they were writing, they saw the school custodian go into the boys' room. A minute later they could hear the sound of hammering. There went their peephole. "I waited a lifetime for that." Jason sighed. "And all I got to see was Cynthia Babcock combing her hair. It's not fair."

Another thing wasn't fair. After first recess Jennifer whispered to Jason that Kelly had changed her mind again. She wasn't playing. "Why not?" asked Jason. Kelly walked by, taking a two-desk detour so she wouldn't have to go near Jason and Benjy. Her eyes flashed sparks. She better be careful, thought Benjy, they could set her papers on fire. "Are you kidding?" said Jennifer. "You have the nerve to ask that? Someone who would stoop so low as to spy on girls in the girls' room? You guys are corroded." And Jennifer marched away, her eyes flashing almost as bright as Kelly's.

Jason shrugged. "Oh, well," he said. "Who needs Kelly? We'll win without her. Right, Benjy?"

"Right," said Benjy.

Just then Mr. Flannagan came back in the room. Benjy quickly opened his human body workbook and started trying to figure out which of those skinny little lines carried the blood from the heart. From now on he was going to listen to every single word that Mr. Flannagan said. *Memorable* had been the word for getting Dictionary. But he never wanted to get it again.

That night Benjy laid out his clothes on his chair once more. He soaked his foot, along with the rest of his body, in the bathtub. It was bath night. Lifting his foot out of the water, he studied its color—a peculiar shade of yellowish green now—and twisted it around every which way. It didn't hurt too much. One good thing about having the game postponed on account of Dictionary, it gave his foot an extra day to get better. It was possible he might be able to run on it tomorrow.

He slept with his playbook under his pillow again. This time he didn't have any dreams. But when he woke up in the morning, it was like a bad dream. His Cowboys sweat shirt and his wristbands were gone.

"Mom!" he yelled, running to the stairs.

His mother was just coming up, a laundry basket in her arms. "It's all right, Benjy," she said. "Don't panic, they're here. Seems like the only time I can get ahold of your clothes to wash them is when you're asleep."

That was a close call. What if the washing machine had broken down or something? He couldn't have played without his Cowboys sweat shirt.

As he put it on he had another thought. This might be the last time he wore it. This time tomorrow Alex's mother might be putting it in her washing machine.

He ate the exact same breakfast as the day before. His father wished him luck again. So did his mother.

"I put a Granola Critter bar in your lunch bag for extra energy," she said. That was big of her. Usually she said Granola Critter bars were junk food. When Benjy went out the door, even his sister said, "Uck." He didn't know if she was talking about his game or her baby cereal.

On the bus Benjy and Jason studied their playbook for the last time.

"You guys planning to show up today?" Adam called from the front of the bus.

"Or maybe you'd rather stay in and copy a little Dictionary," jeered Alex from the back.

"We'll be there," said Jason.

"First recess," said Benjy.

The clock in the classroom moved just as slowly as it had yesterday. Only Benjy wasn't watching it. He kept his eyes glued on Mr. Flannagan. He nodded his head when Mr. Flannagan explained what an adjective was. And he even raised his hand when Mr. Flannagan asked for someone to use an adjective in a sentence. He wasn't taking any chances.

But Mr. Flannagan called on Cynthia Babcock instead.

"Spying on girls in the girls' room is a *terrible* thing," she said. "*Terrible* is an adjective."

Someday he would get back at her for that, Benjy

thought. He looked at her hair. Today she was wearing it in pigtails with funny little pink balls on the ends of them. He imagined taking those pigtails and dipping them in a little peanut butter. But not today.

Mr. Flannagan gave a spelling test, which took up some time. And then Benjy looked up and the clock said 10:42.

Unexpectedly his stomach did a little flipflop. Finally it was time for the fourth-grade Super Bowl. He looked over at Jason. Jason grinned.

"You may put your books away, ladies and gentlemen. And line up for recess."

"Let's go, Benjy," said Jason, jumping out of his chair.

They all got their jackets. Benjy popped half of his Granola Critter bar in his mouth and shoved the other half in his pocket. Extra energy was now speeding through his bloodstream, he hoped.

They met on the lower field. The Flannagan team and the Rinaldi team, face to face. The teams were even—in numbers, anyway. The Flannagan team had Benjy and Jason and Spencer and Danny and Case the Ace and Matthew. The Rinaldi team had Adam and Scott and Eddie Spaghetti and Fernando and Mark Mosquito and Alex. The numbers were all that was even, though. Eddie Spaghetti looked even bigger than Benjy remembered. His shoulders reminded him of a buffalo in the pictures of the Great Plains in his social studies book. Adam was cool and confident, like Johnny Hopkins, the Cowboys quarterback, when Benjy had seen him on a pregame show. And Mark Mosquito, jumping up and down already, seemed as hard to grab on to as a lightning bug. How come he wasn't playing soccer, anyway? He always played soccer these days.

Looking at Alex, strutting around looking as mean as possible, Benjy knew why. Alex had gotten him to play. He wasn't taking any chances about winning this game.

Suddenly Benjy wondered if he and Jason knew what they were doing. What chance did their little *X*'s and *O*'s have against these guys who knew how to play football? What if they wound up just looking silly?

Then Benjy remembered that this was exactly the way things had looked at the beginning of the Cowboys–Seahawks game.

"Hey, Benjy," said Alex softly. "Nice shirt you've got there." The rest of the Rinaldis laughed.

Benjy looked hard at him. "Thanks," he said just as softly. "I like it too."

Adam and Jason were arguing about the toss of the coin.

"Come on, let's go," said Danny.

"Yeah," said Eddie Spaghetti. "You're wasting time." He dug a quarter out of his jeans. "I'll toss it, you call it," he said to Jason.

Jason called heads. It was tails. The Flannagan team had to kick off.

These guys did know how to play football. Benjy could see it right away. They must have been practicing a lot. They played like a well-oiled machine, running over everything in their path. First Eddie Spaghetti knocked everyone over. Then Fernando ran through the holes. Or Mark Mosquito darted around end, leaving six tacklers grabbing at the air. Then, when the Flannagan team was looking for Mark or Fernando, Adam dumped off a little pass to Alex. Or tossed a long one to Scott. His passes were always right on target. The Rinaldi machine kept rolling. The Flannagan team couldn't seem to stop them. In five plays they had a touchdown.

"Yessirree, Benjy-baby," gloated Alex as they lined up for the kickoff. "I sure do like that shirt."

Benjy didn't say anything.

Danny took the kickoff and ran it back to the bush with the red berries, which they figured was the twenty yard line. Not a bad runback. But they had eighty yards to go for a score.

The Flannagan team went into a huddle.

"Okay, guys, this is it," said Jason, grinning like mad. "Boy, wait till they see what we've got up our sleeve."

Benjy wished he was as sure as Jason that this was going to work. Past Spencer he could see Eddie Spaghetti crouched at the line of scrimmage. With his huge shoulders hunched and his dark hair in his eyes, he looked just like a buffalo. A ten-ton buffalo.

"Twenty-two-X," said Jason. "On a quick count. Those guys aren't going to know what hit them."

Twenty-two-X was the lateral play. Benjy to Danny, going back the other way. If they did it right, it could really surprise the Rinaldi team.

The Flannagans lined up. "Fifty-two," started Jason slowly. Then, suddenly, "Hike!"

He shoved the ball into Benjy's hands. Benjy took off, around right end. The Rinaldi team was slow going after him. The quick count had fooled them. Benjy got past Fernando and Scott. He was to the thirty yard line. But his foot slowed him down. Alex and Mark were closing in on him.

Benjy glanced behind him. There was Danny, just where he was supposed to be. Mark was about to push Benjy out of bounds. He lateraled the ball.

Danny had it. He reversed across the field. No one was there, since they'd all gone to the right side with

Benjy. Only Adam was chasing him. And Danny could outrun Adam any day.

He was at the Rinaldi forty. Thirty. Twenty. Ten. Touchdown!

Jason pulled Benjy to his feet. He and Spencer and Case the Ace and Matthew pounded each other on the back. "I knew it would work!" said Jason.

Inside his head Benjy heard the TV announcer saying, "And the Flannagan team is right back in this ball game!"

The Rinaldi team sure looked as if they didn't know what hit them. Suddenly Eddie Spaghetti didn't seem so big. And Adam didn't seem so cool. And when they lined up for the kickoff, Alex didn't say a word about Benjy's shirt.

But they pulled themselves together pretty fast. Mark Mosquito took the kickoff, and it looked like he was going all the way. He zipped past Danny, stepped around Matthew, and dodged Benjy's grasping hands like a breeze blowing by. Spencer was chasing him at midfield. He just barely got a hand on him, slowing Mark down enough for Case the Ace to bring him down at last. But he was on the Flannagan five. On the next play Eddie Spaghetti just put his head down like a charging buffalo and plowed through for the score.

Alex was grinning again.

Benjy was worried. If they couldn't stop the Rinaldi offense, they weren't going to win the game in spite of all their trick plays. That had been the Seahawks problem. That was why they finally lost to the Cowboys. The Flannagan team was going to have to come up with some defense.

Jason was still confident, though. "Fifty-six-J!" he whispered excitedly in the huddle. "Slow count. This one's going to kill them."

It was his favorite, the hidden ball trick.

They lined up. The Rinaldi team looked wide awake, ready for a quick count.

"Sixty-four!" barked Jason. "Thirty-one! Ninety-nine, sixteen, forty-three, seventy-five, thirty-six!" He paused for breath. The Rinaldi team was looking at him like he'd lost his marbles. "Fifty-seven, twenty, sixty-four, eighty-eight—hike!"

Jason faked a handoff to Spencer. Spencer started right, his arms folded where the ball should be. Benjy was right behind him. He ran left, his arms folded where the ball should be. Danny was behind him, his arms the same way. And Case the Ace. And Matthew.

Mark tackled Spencer at the line of scrimmage. Alex nailed Benjy. And Eddie Spaghetti went for Danny. Meanwhile Jason, with the ball hidden behind his hip, cruised all the way to the Rinaldi twenty yard line before Adam noticed him and brought him down.

"How was that for a play? Oh, I love it! Did you see their faces? They didn't know who to tackle." Jason bounced up and down in the huddle. "What shall we give them now?" he asked. "How about a little razzle-dazzle forty-seven-T?"

Benjy had a sudden thought. "That's what they'll be expecting," he said. "They think all our plays are going to be tricky now. So how about a little straight pass? Case in the end zone?"

Jason tapped his finger on his forehead. "Good thinking, Benjy."

The play worked. The Rinaldis were so busy worrying about quick counts and slow counts and who had the ball that Case had it in the end zone before they knew what had happened. It was tie score.

Now was the time for the Flannagan defense to get tough. They couldn't let the Rinaldis score again. Time was running out. And there was no overtime at recess.

"Okay, guys," said Jason. "We need the ball. Any way we can get it. Intercept a pass, make them fumble, don't let them get a first down—anything."

That was a big order, the way the Rinaldis were

playing. But all of a sudden Benjy had a feeling that they could do it.

"How about each of us taking a man and sticking to him? Don't let him move," he said. "I'll take Mark."

"I've got Fernando," said Danny.

"I can stop Eddie Spaghetti," said Matthew. "I think."

"You can," said Jason. "You're bigger than he is. Case, you cover Scott, and Spencer, you stick with Adam. I'll take care of Alex."

On the first play Eddie Spaghetti carried the ball. He came crashing through the line, knocking over Jason and Danny. His buffalo shoulders met Matthew's. For a minute neither one budged an inch. Then Matthew shoved with all his weight. Eddie Spaghetti was thrown for a one-yard loss.

"All *right*!" said Jason, punching Matthew in the arm. "That's using the old muscles."

The next play would probably be Mark Mosquito around end. Unless Adam tried a pass. Benjy got ready. He crouched down, his eyes fastened on Mark. He wasn't going anywhere without Benjy. Benjy's foot didn't hurt anymore. He could keep up with Mark, he knew he could.

Mark shifted his feet. That was a giveaway, Benjy

suddenly realized. He was going to carry the ball. Just as it was snapped, Benjy leaped at him. Eddie Spaghetti tried to block, but Benjy just managed to grab Mark's foot. Mark was stopped for no gain.

Now it was third down. This was the big one. If the Rinaldis didn't make a first down this time, they would have to punt and the Flannagans would take over. With his eyes Benjy measured the distance from the line of scrimmage to the sewer pipe, the first-down marker. It was a good eleven yards, maybe twelve. The Rinaldi team would have to pass.

"Watch the pass," Benjy muttered to Case. He nodded and nudged Jason and Spencer. "Pass," he whispered.

Adam took the snap and faded back. It was a pass play. He looked for a receiver. But Case was covering Scott deep, and Jason was waving his arms in front of Alex. Mark Mosquito jumped around, trying to get free. But Benjy was with him at every step.

Adam faded back some more. Still no one was free. Then all of a sudden someone was on top of Adam, smothering the ball, crushing him to the ground. Benjy couldn't believe it. It was Matthew. He'd gotten past Eddie Spaghetti.

Matthew got up, waving his fists in the air and doing a little dance. "I got a sack!" he yelled. "Did you see that? A real sack!"

It was a big loss, all the way back to the Rinaldi thirty yard line. Now they had to punt for sure.

Scott boomed a long one, almost to the Flannagan end zone. Spencer caught it, but he was tackled right away by Fernando. So the Flannagan team had the ball. Only they were deep in their own territory. Ninety yards away from the winning touchdown. And recess was nearly over. It had to be.

"We've got to move the ball," said Danny. "Fast."

"No problem," said Jason. "We'll give them good old forty-seven-T."

That was the play where Spencer ran the ball, then tossed a surprise pass to Case the Ace.

It worked perfectly. Spencer started running on a slant to the left. Then, just as he was about to be tackled by Fernando, he threw a pass. It was a pretty wobbly throw, but no one was there except Case the Ace, and he got all the way to the Rinaldi thirty before he was tackled. It was a sixty-yard gain.

Next they tried a regular play, Danny up the middle. It worked too. The Rinaldis were off-balance, looking for something fancy. Danny gained sixteen yards for another first down.

"And now fifty-six-J again," said Jason. "What do you bet I score without anyone laying a single hand on me?"

But the Rinaldis weren't falling for the hidden ball

trick again. Mark had Jason around the ankles before Benjy and Danny had taken a single step. No gain.

The Flannagan team went back in the huddle. Out of the corner of his eye, Benjy could see Mrs. Bloom, the teacher on recess duty, walking toward the door. That meant the bell would be ringing any minute. There was time for just one more play.

The ball was on the fourteen yard line.

"How about twenty-two-X again?" said Jason.

"They'll spot it," said Case the Ace.

"Fourteen-Q?"

That was where Jason and Benjy switched places and Jason ended up catching the ball.

"Too risky," said Benjy. He was afraid of throwing an interception to end the game.

"Hey, what about my play?" said Matthew.

Benjy and Jason looked at each other. They'd almost forgotten. That was the one to try. But could Matthew go fourteen yards before the Rinaldi team caught on and dragged him down? Fourteen yards suddenly seemed like a very long way.

"Please," pleaded Matthew. "I can do it."

Maybe he could.

"Okay," said Jason. "We'll give them the quick count and then eighty-eight-M. Matt, put your head down and go."

Spencer took Matthew's place at center. Before the Rinaldis had a chance to wonder about that, Jason called, "Sixty-three—hike!" And he jammed the ball into Matthew's stomach.

Matthew crashed forward. Spencer and Danny were blocking Eddie Spaghetti aside. Mark dove at Matthew's legs, but he couldn't bring him down. Adam tackled him from one side and Fernando from the other.

But Matthew kept rolling. He was at about the seven yard line. Now Alex was jumping on his back. And Eddie Spaghetti too. Matthew was going down. On the five yard line.

"Matt!" yelled Benjy suddenly. "Lateral!"

Just as Matthew went down, he managed to toss the ball in the air. It was anybody's ball. Danny jumped for it. So did Scott. And Danny had it. He was heading for the end zone.

But then somehow Eddie Spaghetti had him around the ankles. Danny struggled desperately to get free. But he couldn't. He was going down. On the two yard line.

"Danny!" said Benjy. "Here!"

Danny flipped the ball backward. Benjy got one hand on it. For a terrible moment he juggled it in the air. And then he had it in both hands.

He jumped over a tangle of fallen bodies. And he was in the end zone. Standing up. With the winning touchdown.

Benjy held the ball up high over his head, then slammed it down in his best Billy Joe Crockett style. And then he was surrounded by the Flannagan team.

13

The Flannagan team couldn't believe they'd actually won the fourth-grade Super Bowl. All day they went around grinning and punching each other in the arm and telling each other how great they'd played.

"That sure was quick thinking on that last play," Jason said to Benjy.

"Thanks," said Benjy. "Nice lateral," he said to Danny.

"Terrific catches," Danny said to Case the Ace.

"Boy, that was some run," Case the Ace said to Matthew.

"What about my sack?" asked Matthew.

Even Kelly Kramer congratulated the Flannagan

team. "I never thought you could do it," she told Jason. For some reason this made Benjy feel best of all.

The Rinaldi team couldn't believe they'd lost. They walked around in a state of shock, complaining.

"It was a fluke," said Adam.

"Yeah," said Scott. "You guys tricked us."

"I bet that last play wasn't even legal," grumbled Alex.

By second recess, though, they were asking for a rematch.

"No way," said Jason. "That was the Super Bowl. There aren't any more games after the Super Bowl."

"Yeah," said Benjy. "It's the end of the season."

"It's only November," Adam pointed out. "And this isn't the NFL, it's the fourth grade. What are you going to do at recess, play soccer?"

"Yes," said Benjy and Jason together.

And they did, at second recess. Benjy didn't like soccer that much. And it *was* only November. Most likely they'd have to have a rematch. But they didn't have to have it right away. They could enjoy being Super Bowl champs for a little while.

After school a Cowboys football helmet mysteriously appeared on Benjy's front steps. The doorbell rang, but no one was there but the helmet. "That's strange," said Benjy's mother, looking puzzled. "How do you suppose that got there?"

"It's for me," said Benjy, smiling. So Alex had kept his part of the deal. He hadn't been so sure he would.

Benjy ran upstairs and tried it on. The helmet fit him just right. And it was a professional model too, the kind he'd seen in the sports store. He went to the mirror and checked it out. With the helmet and his Cowboys sweat shirt and his wristbands, now he looked exactly like the magazine picture of Billy Joe Crockett on his bulletin board. In case Billy Joe had a little injury sometime, Benjy could run out on the field and take his place.

"How do I look, Clyde?" he asked.

Clyde stared at him through the side of the bowl. For a minute he didn't move a single fin. Even his mouth was still.

"I agree," said Benjy. "Totally awesome."

He had to do his homework, but he didn't exactly feel like it. He sat down at his desk with his helmet still on and stared at his math workbook. Fractions —yuck.

After a minute he got out his library book instead, the one called *Heroes of the NFL Today.* Someday he might be in a book like this himself. Because he was going to be a football star when he grew up, no matter what Charlie Fryhoffer said. He'd grow. Or if he didn't, he'd just run around and between and under those big guys.

Or maybe, in case for some reason he didn't grow, he'd be a quarterback. Bart Thorn wasn't very big, he'd noticed, and he'd almost beaten the Cowboys all by himself. It was okay to be small if you were a quarterback because you had all those giant linemen to protect you. And a quarterback got to think up all kinds of great plays. That would be fun. Of course, he'd have to work on his passing. His arm wasn't quite ready for the NFL.

His head was, though. Even Jason thought so. After the game he'd given Benjy a nickname. Finally. And Matthew too. He called Matt The Incredible Hulk. And Benjy was The Bionic Brain.

Benjy couldn't get his bionic brain to work on fractions. Finally he gave up. He got his football from the closet and went out to the backyard.

He played the entire fourth-grade Super Bowl game all over again, acting out every play. He started with the first lateral play, Benjy to Danny. Then he ran through the hidden ball trick, playing all the parts. And the halfback surprise pass, and Matthew's surprise sack of Adam. He ended with the last game-winning lateral play, Matthew to Danny to Benjy for the score.

He did an instant replay of that last one a few times,

just so he'd never forget it. He'd really done it. His quick thinking had won the game for the Flannagan team.

He practiced doing a little dance in the end zone, like he'd seen players on TV do when they scored. Then he went back inside.

"Did you see that?" he asked his mother. "That was my game-winning play."

"Very impressive," said his mother.

"Preff," said his sister.

It flashed across Benjy's bionic brain that he was hungry. He'd forgotten to have his snack. He couldn't expect to grow if he didn't eat every chance he got.

He poured himself a big bowl of Zingies with banana slices on top and sat down at the table. His mother and Melissa joined him for some apple juice.

It was a little hard to eat with his helmet on. He had trouble getting the spoon through the chin guard. But he did it.

"Mom," he said. "Did I tell you about my game-winning play?"

"Several times," said his mother.

"Oh," said Benjy. "How about the halfback surprise pass? And the hidden ball trick? Did I tell you about those?"

His mother nodded. "Those too."

"And the way we did quick counts and long counts to mix them up?" said Benjy. "That was my idea too, you know."

"I know," said his mother. "That was really using the old brain."

"Well," said Benjy, "do you have any questions?"

Benjy's mother seemed to be thinking it over, looking into her glass of apple juice. "As a matter of fact," she said finally, "I do have one."

"What is it?" asked Benjy.

"Are you planning to sleep in that helmet?"

Benjy grinned, working a big bite of banana through the chin guard. "As a matter of fact," he said, "I am."

About the Author

Jean Van Leeuwen is the author of many books for young readers, including *Benjy in Business, Benjy and the Power of Zingies,* and *The Great Rescue Operation.* She has also written four Easy-to-Read* books, most recently *Tales of Amanda Pig.*

Ms. Van Leeuwen was raised in Rutherford, New Jersey, and attended Syracuse University. She has worked as a children's book editor in New York City and currently lives in Chappaqua, New York, with her husband and two children.

About the Artist

Gail Owens has illustrated over fifty children's books, most recently *Julia's Magic.* Born in Detroit, she now lives in Rock Tavern, New York.